# BOOK ON

# THE ISLE

## STUART JAFFE

Copyright © 2018 by Stuart Jaffe
Cover art by Deranged Doctor Design

ISBN 13: 978-1985778443
ISBN 10: 1985778440

First Edition: March, 2018
Second Edition: October, 2019

For Glory

# Also by Stuart Jaffe

*Max Porter Paranormal Mysteries*
Southern Bound      Southern Curses      Southern Fury
Southern Charm      Southern Rites       Southern Souls
Southern Belle      Southern Craft
Southern Gothic     Southern Spirit
Southern Haunts     Southern Flames

*Nathan K Thrillers*                    *Parallel Society*
Immortal Killers                        The Infinity Caverns
Killing Machine                         Book on the Isle
The Cardinal                            Rift Angel
Yukon Massacre                          Lost Time
The First Battle
Immortal Darkness
A Spy for Eternity
Prisoner
Desert Takedown

*The Malja Chronicles*
The Way of the Black Beast
The Way of the Sword and Gun
The Way of the Brother Gods
The Way of the Blade
The Way of the Power
The Way of the Soul

*Stand Alone Novels*                    *Gillian Boone Novels*
After The Crash                         A Glimpse of Her Soul
Real Magic                              Pathway to Spirit
Founders

*Short Story Collection*
10 Bits of My Brain           10 More Bits of My Brain
The Marshall Drummond Case Files: Cabinet 1
The Bluesman

*Non-Fiction*
How to Write Magical Words: A Writer's Companion

# BOOK ON

# THE ISLE

# CHAPTER 1

Veronica "Roni" Rider sat in the breakfast nook of Elliot and Sully's apartment. Living on the fifth floor of the *In The Bind* bookstore, the two old men had been part of her family for decades. Along with Gram, they made up all that Roni had left. Which made her problem all the more difficult.

"You should talk to her," Sully said, pushing his glasses up his nose. He scratched at the white tufts that ringed his head. "She's your grandmother, after all, and that's important."

Elliot laughed — a powerful sound that denied his age. With exacting motions, he scrambled eggs in a small pan. "We are talking about Lillian, correct? Roni's Gram?"

"Phooey, to you. Yes, of course, Gram can be prickly about things at times, but this is her granddaughter and the future of the Parallel Society."

Roni had been joining the boys for breakfast most every day for the last year — ever since she had discovered the truth about the Old Gang. Lillian "Gram" Donaugh, Elliot Kenwana, and Sully Greenbaum were no ordinary trio of elderly folk. Not at all. They had been saving the universe for decades.

"That's my problem," Roni said. "What kind of future will the Society have when all Gram will let me do is library work?"

Sully wagged a finger. "You're our researcher, our librarian. Where else should you work? I make Golems, so I work in the studio with the clay. Gram's gifts are the chains and books that bind the tears between universes — that's why her office is the entrance to the caverns that house all those books. And Elliot — well, his abilities don't really get an office here."

Elliot laughed louder than before. "If I was not healing you every few months, you would have died ages ago. Besides, I do not think Roni is complaining about her work environment." Though Elliot had been an American citizen for over twenty years, his Kenyan birth and London upbringing made his speech exact and his insights worldly. "It is more the work itself, yes?"

Accepting a plate of eggs, Roni tucked into her food — easier to focus on eating than on the truth of Elliot's words. "I don't want to seem ungrateful."

As Elliot settled at the small table, Sully rose and went about pouring mugs of coffee for the three of them. "Nobody'll think you're ungrateful. You want more responsibility. That's admirable. Shows real chutzpah. And you should get it, too. You need to learn more about what we do so that you'll be ready when the time comes."

"That is absolutely right," Elliot said. "Because Gram and Sully and I have our powers, you might be mistakenly thinking that we have magic over life and death. But this is not true. We are mortal, and we are old."

"Listen to him. Elliot's done a marvelous job of healing Gram and me for years, but we all die eventually. You have to be ready to take over."

Roni set down her fork. "Then help me talk with her. If the only other members of the Parallel Society support me, then she'll have to listen."

Elliot twitched his eye towards Sully. "That would not be advisable."

"He's right," Sully said and slurped some coffee, hiding his eyes behind the mug. "In fact, Gram will only dig her heels in deeper if we get involved."

Roni shook her head and chuckled. "Cowards."

"No," Sully said. "We're simply smart. Trust me. When she's ready, she'll ask us our opinions and then we'll support you. But to do more will only get you less."

Roni pushed away from the table with a firm motion. "You're right. How can I go about learning to save the universe, if I can't even approach my grandmother with a simple request to have more responsibility in this outfit?"

"What? Now?"

"Why not? She'll be up. Heck, she'll be downstairs already, probably going through the bookstore inventory to see what to order."

Sully gazed at the refrigerator. "I haven't even toasted my bagel yet."

Leaning over, Roni kissed the top of Sully's head. "Enjoy your breakfast, boys. I've got to go chat with Gram."

Elliot patted her arm. "You will do fine. And when we come downstairs, if we must, we will clean your blood from the floor as if it never had been spilled."

Roni and Sully stared at him in shock. But then Elliot's face broke into a wide grin, and all three laughed. For Roni, though, the nervous energy beneath their mirth cut straight into her chest.

She took the elevator to the first floor, its close confines like a coffin pressing in. When it came to rest with a hard bump, she considered opening the panel that housed the button for the secret floors beneath the building. She could simply go down to the Grand Library and get to work.

No. She had to deal with Gram. A year was more than enough time. Too much, in fact.

Walking toward the front of the bookstore reminded her that she had grown up here. The smell of the old books, the feel of the narrow aisles, the sound of the hushed voices — from the baseboard molding that she had carved her initials into when she turned fourteen to the dent in the metal shelves of the Fantasy section where she had smacked her head after running (and falling) at age seven — every inch of the place belonged to her childhood. She knew it all.

Or she thought she did. Until she learned of the endless caverns beneath, the secret rooms on secret floors, and that her Gram and the Old Gang were powerful heroes battling amazing worlds, she had really known nothing about the place.

Gram manned the front counter with a large ledger open before her. Though not an all-out technophobe, Gram insisted on doing the books by hand. A stout woman, she kept one hand following the ledger numbers and the other clenching her beaded, crucifix necklace that sat on the shelf of her prominent chest.

Lifting her head, she nodded. "Good morning, Roni."

"Morning."

Roni's legs weakened. She could still turn toward the basement stairs and catch the elevator one floor below. But Gram would wonder why she had taken such an odd route. If Gram didn't stop her to ask then, the question would arise later in the day.

The OPEN sign hung in the doorway, but nobody would bother coming inside for a few more hours. It was a rare day that anybody arrived before ten o'clock. So, Roni couldn't use customers as an excuse.

"Something on your mind?" Gram asked.

Roni trembled a smile. She had been standing still long enough to be noticeable. In fact, she realized, she stood next to the big table — a large, square oak table that ruled over the center reading area of the store. Many of the big conversations in her life had happened at this table — starting with the first big one, the day Gram told Roni that her mother had died in a car accident and that her father had been institutionalized.

"I haven't all day," Gram said. "What's this about?"

"Well," Roni said, and to her surprise, her voice sounded firm.

"Well what?"

"It's been a year since I've learned the truth about you and the world and everything. I've spent this year in the sub-basement, cleaning up the library, organizing the books and maps and all of it, and that's been fine."

Gram straightened. "But?"

"It's time I get more involved. I need more responsibilities. I need to learn how to do everything so that I'm ready."

"And what exactly do you mean by *everything?* You want to go out fighting creatures with us?"

"Yes. But also, I should be introduced to the various contacts you have. I know there are religious leaders and other people all over the world who report to you when they spot trouble. How are they going to know to call me when ... that is ..."

"When I die?"

"I've done my year of penance. Shouldn't I be allowed to join the Society in full?"

With a firm snap — a well-honed maneuver — Gram closed the ledger. Roni lowered to the nearest chair at the big table. Her mouth dried.

"Let me understand this," Gram said, and Roni's throat closed up. "You've decided that after a measly year, that you deserve to become a full member of the Parallel Society — the most important group in this entire universe, the one group of people protecting everybody. The fact that I'm the leader means nothing to you."

"I only meant —"

Gram put up a hand to silence Roni. "You think because you've decided that you're bored with the task I gave you, that your penance, as you put it, should be over. Let's look at what caused your penance. You brought a date into this building and let him discover the hidden caverns."

"I didn't let him do anything. I didn't even know about any of that stuff at the time."

"Nonetheless, you knew that nobody was allowed in my office, but you allowed him —"

"He broke in."

"Under you guard."

"I wasn't a damn sentry."

"Watch your language." Gram stepped out from behind the counter and loomed larger. "After we rescued the man, Darin, from the book he fell into, you were supposed to get rid of him. Instead, you ended up — unwittingly again — aiding him into become stronger and more of a problem. Finally, with Elliot and Sully's help, we stopped Darin from potentially enslaving our world. And we all almost died doing so. During that time, you couldn't make up your mind if you wanted to join us. When you finally decided to be part of the team, I made it clear that you had no special powers other than your mind. You're smart and you love books. This makes you ideal to be our team researcher. I figured with all the journals and reports from centuries of the Society's existence at your fingertips, you'd be enjoying all there was to learn for several years to come. Penance? That was a gift."

"Meanwhile, you three are doing the real job of the Society and you never once call upon me for help. The idea that I'm your team researcher is a joke."

Gram marched to the edge of the table. Her stern glower lightened. "Is that what you think?"

"Just last week, you and Sully went off to Argentina, and two months ago, you sent Elliot to Poland."

"Dear, the reason we haven't called for your help on jobs is because there haven't been any. Those trips were more about keeping strong network ties with those that help us. It's a big world, so every bit of help is appreciated. But going a year without trouble is not unheard of. Longest we've gone was five years, and I'm sure some of the Society members from centuries past went even longer. Other universes crashing into ours is not a weekly event. Thank the Lord for that."

Roni frowned. The idea that she had not been excluded left her in doubt. She wanted to believe Gram, but that proved harder all the time. After all, Gram had lied to Roni from as far back as she could remember. No matter how much justification she wanted to grant Gram, the lies remained. Clearly, nothing as threatening as Darin had occurred in the last year, but nothing at all?

Clinging to her anger, Roni said, "That might be, but I still need to meet the people that you network with. I still need to know more about how to do any of this job. If a meteor strikes tomorrow and kills you three off, then I barely know anything. The Parallel Society would be ruined."

"It's a good thing there are no apocalyptic meteors on the way."

"Joking isn't going to change my mind."

Gram's gentle smile turned into a thin line. "Nor mine. You have an important job to do, but allow me to be clear — you work for us. Not the other way around. The Parallel Society has been operating far longer than we have written records for, and there is a method to keeping the whole thing going. So, stop worrying about yourself and how all this affects you, and start working for all of us."

"That's not at all what —"

"Enough of this. I'm all upset now. Please mind the store until the boys come down. I'm going to my apartment for a rest. When I return, I hope to find you in the Grand Library where you belong."

Without waiting for Roni's response, Gram shuffled toward the elevator. Her apartment took up the other half of the fifth floor opposite Elliot and Sully. Roni waited until the elevator closed before she punched down on the table. The smack's dull echo died around her leaving a lonely silence.

"Well, shit," she said.

# CHAPTER 2

Roni spent the remainder of the day working as usual —
sifting through old journals, organizing ancient books and
diaries, taking scraps of hand-drawn maps and attempting
to make sense of the twisting, winding caverns beneath her.
But unlike her usual workdays, her thoughts did not fill up
with the wonder of the library. Instead, she replayed her
conversation with Gram.

*More like a lecture.*

No matter what angle she looked at it, Roni returned to
the same result — Gram did not trust her. Gram had kept
the truth of the universe hidden despite knowing that at
some point Roni would have to take over. She had kept the
gang's current cases secret, claiming that nothing had
happened in the last year. She had kept Roni isolated in the
library, away from all the other secrets she must be holding.

By the time the day ended, Roni had worked herself into
a quiet rage. She tramped out of the bookstore without a
word to anybody and headed to the 1st Street Bar. After
two shots of whiskey and a beer, she relaxed enough to take
a cab to Cody's Saloon. Several more drinks and she found
her way to Nicki's Corner. By that point, midnight had

come around. That's when she met Frank.

Young, fit, and handsome — though she had enough sense to question if he really looked that way or if the alcohol had made him that way. He bought her a beer. "It's late for a girl to be drinking on a Wednesday night."

"Late for anybody," she said.

He smiled and her body tingled. "Very true."

With that auspicious introduction, she spent the next hour chatting away about movies and television shows. She wondered if he read books — one of the few passions in her life — but reminded herself not to care about him in that way. There would be no more romantic relationships in her life. How could there be? She had a monumental secret. If she got close enough to a man that she might reveal the truth about the world, she would put that man's life at risk. Darin died because of that secret, and they had only dated twice.

"Frank," she said, interrupting his observations on the comedy of *Seinfeld,* "there are only two reasons people are drinking hard in a bar on a Wednesday night. Either they're a drunk or they're looking to get laid. I'm not a drunk."

Roni followed the cracks along the bedroom ceiling as she listened to the gentle snoring of the stranger beside her. Dim light peeked through the window blinds. Morning would arrive soon. Much of the previous night blurred together, but she knew enough. She drank too much, met up with Frank, and topped the night off in his bed. Twice.

With a gentle motion, she rocked her head from shoulder to shoulder. No pounding pain. No blistering fire from the sounds of the rustling pillowcase. Other than some dehydration, she fared well. No major hangover. If she were religious like any of the Old Gang, she would thank the Lord for small favors. As it was, she merely marveled at her body's resilience.

After a few minutes, she jiggled the mattress but Frank continued to snore. Good. Peeling back the white-and-gray striped comforter, she eased her legs free. The floor chilled her feet and she involuntarily hissed. Autumn in Pennsylvania could create some brisk mornings. Holding still a moment, she waited until she heard the snoring resume. A few breaths later, she rolled off the mattress and onto her feet.

Rising on her tiptoes, she leaned over enough to see the side of his face — not bad looking, certainly nothing to be horrified by. She had done worse.

Throwing on last night's clothes, she padded in bare feet across the apartment. Like a thief in reverse, she slipped out to the hall and eased the apartment door shut so that the lock made a meek click. Sitting in the stairwell, she put on her socks and shoes, stuffed her bra into her handbag, and checked her cellphone — 7:02 am. She hurried downstairs, out the building's front door, and fast-walked her way along the broken sidewalk on Arbor Street.

She had not been in the northwestern part of Olburg in years, but she recalled a corner diner a few blocks over — the Olburg Chestnut. Inhaling slow and deep, letting the cool morning air fill her lungs and clear her head, she eased her pace. As she neared the corner, she knew the old eatery remained — she could smell the frying bacon and fresh coffee. A hard-looking lot shuffled their way into the diner — truck drivers, road crews, and other blue collar men and women seeking a hearty start to their day. None of the business suits came here. They all grabbed a donut and coffee on their commute to Philadelphia. The people here were those that kept the local world running.

Except one man.

He wore a pressed suit, leaned on a black cane with a silver handle, and played with his mustache styled from the 1920s. Though he merely waited on the sidewalk, Roni's instincts kicked in — she had no doubt that the man waited for her. As she neared, his head jerked in her direction, and he fashioned a dark grin.

"Ms. Veronica Rider? Yes?"

He had a smooth voice with an odd accent — not one she could place to any particular country. She brushed by him and entered the diner.

The hustle of waitresses blended with the chimes of silverware and the sizzling of the griddle. Laughter, mumbled conversation, and the call of food orders drifted along heavy aromas of pancakes and eggs. A sign up front stated: *Please seat yourself.* Only problem: no seats available.

Standing at the door with the cold air from outside fighting the warmth of the diner, Roni scanned around for signs of anybody about the leave. The odd man from outside entered behind her and stood quietly. Like a passenger on a sinking ship, she searched again for a table to save her. Nothing.

Refusing to look back, she said, "You a lawyer?"

As if insulted, he said, "Never."

"Good. Thought you might be serving a summons."

Two men wearing jackets with *Stoltzfus Plumbing* on the backs tossed some cash on their table and walked off. Roni nabbed their booth near the back and waited as a young man hustled to bus the table. Once he left, another young man set the table with paper placemats (complete with ads for local businesses), silverware wrapped in paper napkins, and two thick coffee mugs. The man in the nice suit settled in opposite Roni. She thought about making a scene, but that required too much energy. Instead, she nudged her mug toward the aisle, and as if by magic, a waitress walked by and filled it with hot caffeinated goodness.

"You want something to eat?" the waitress asked.

Roni didn't bother looking up. "Two eggs, over easy, and some toast."

"And you, sir?"

"Nothing, thank you."

Once the waitress left, the man unrolled his napkin and set about placing his knife, fork, and spoon in the proper positions. Roni sipped her coffee. Under other circumstances, she would have told the guy to go away. If he refused, she could easily get one of the many strong men to escort the guy out of the diner — probably throw a few punches, too. But that morning, she wanted to simply sip her coffee, find her way home, and curl into her own bed. Her body needed to recalibrate.

But then the man spoke again. This time, his voice deepened, and the words he said spun the world around her head. "We need to talk about the multiverse, your grandmother, and the rest of the Parallel Society."

# CHAPTER 3

The incessant rumble of the busy diner ceased. The clatter of dishes, the chimes of the main door opening, the conversations muddling together, the cellphones beeping and singing and chirping — all of it simply disappeared as if somebody had forgotten to add sound to the picture. Roni stared at the well-dressed man opposite her as the coffee in her stomach threatened to return.

"What did you say?" she finally managed, and with those words life around her returned to normal volumes.

"Oh, yes, I'm well aware of the truth. Surely, your grandmother explained that there were many of us out there in the world who had learned — or, at least, had believed. Not many as in thousands or such, but certainly more than a few. Perhaps a hundred or so. Maybe less."

"Must have slipped her mind."

"Well, then, allow me to be direct so as to avoid further confusions."

Roni lowered her hand beneath the table and clenched a fist. She didn't know if she wanted to punch this guy or turn her anger upon Gram. Instead, she listened.

"My name is Kenneth Bay. I am the current emissary of

the being Yal-hara."

"*The being?*"

Kenneth raised his pointer finger. "Please. Permit me to finish before you ask questions. It will save time." He waited until Roni sat back and gestured for him to continue. Stroking his mustache as he exhaled, he went on, "Thank you. Yal-hara is from another universe. One night, a tear in her world opened beneath her while she slept, and it deposited her in our world. Until that moment she knew nothing of the multiverse. She was a teacher, actually. She instructed the young in basic skills — what we call reading, writing, and arithmetic.

"This all occurred in the year 1907 in the Sahara Desert. She nearly died, but a nomadic tribe came upon her and took her into their care. When the Parallel Society of that time arrived and captured the rift into one of their books, Yal-hara was twenty miles away and being treated like a god. It would take her many years to find her way out of the desert, learn enough languages to survive, and create a source of wealth — all the while keeping hidden from mankind."

"Why hidden?"

"No interruptions, please. However, to answer your question — not all beings that come here can pass as human. Eventually, Yal-hara learned of the Society — this was in 1932. At that time, they were using Paris as their homebase. She sent her emissary to contact the Society, and it did not go well. They attempted to assassinate her. I suppose they thought that the most prudent course of action — dispose of the problem. But their rash decision drove her into deeper hiding."

Roni opened her mouth but held back her next question. She opted for a sip of coffee, though she doubted Kenneth Bay had been fooled.

"By 1944, Yal-hara had settled in America. Turned out that the turmoil Hitler had caused also created enough chaos to benefit her travels. Nobody bothered her. The war took the lives of all but one member of the Society. That woman, Grace Covington, relocated to Philadelphia — no easy feat when you consider the dangers of moving all those books. Eventually, she met your grandmother and passed the torch. Yal-hara spent her days educating herself on the world and learning all she could about the multiverse. But, of course, that subject is not widely known, and she could not easily approach your Gram, as I believe you call her. After the Parallel Society had reformed to its full complement, Yal-hara decided to risk exposing her existence. She sent her newest emissary, my father, but unfortunately, the meeting did not go well. The Society made it clear that they had little interest in Yal-hara's story and only wanted to send her back into the multiverse — any book would do. Though better than before — after all, your Gram did not attempt to kill Yal-hara — they still did not want to help solve the actual problem. This was unacceptable. Yal-hara had learned enough about the mulitverse to know that some of the worlds were dark and terrible places."

Roni shuddered as she recalled gazing into the open book Darin had fallen inside. It stretched downward like an esophagus while anguished creatures wrenched their bodies against the membrane wall. At the bottom, she saw hurricanes blasting across while thunder cracked the air. It had been enough to destroy Darin's sanity.

"Once again, Yal-hara went into hiding. However, she always maintained an eye upon the Society. It was then, and remains now, her only real hope. But she is growing old, and with that, her desperation grows, too. I took over from my father as her emissary, and against my advice, she attempted to infiltrate the caverns through Darin Lander. You are quite aware of the results."

"So that was all you?"

"Not me. Yal-hara. And while the entire endeavor was regrettable, the one positive was your inclusion into the Society. After careful observations, Yal-hara and I both agreed that you represent a new and much needed perspective on the Society — one worth reaching out to for help. That's precisely why I am here. She has waited a long time for someone like you — someone caring and open-minded. Can you imagine how hard it must have been to live for over a century as the only fully-sentient, non-human being on this planet? And please, don't bring up chimpanzees. I know they're sentient, but they are mindless twits compared to Yal-hara. All she asks is a small favor that will help her immensely."

"Sure. Because everything you've told me leads to a *small* favor."

Kenneth laced his fingers as he rested his arms on the table. "You're wary. It's only natural. You should be. The only thing that lends credence to my words is the fact that I say them at all, that I am aware of the Society and the books and the caverns and Darin and the rest of it, but why should that be enough?"

Roni couldn't tell if he mocked her. Before she snapped out a response, he sighed and pulled a torn piece of paper from his coat. Her eyes widened. On the table, sitting between her half-eaten eggs and a mug of coffee, Kenneth had placed a map fragment depicting part of the caverns.

"How did you get this?" she asked.

"Yal-hara gave it to me to give to you. I never questioned how she acquired it. I assume that if one lives as long as she does, enough things happen that one ends up with all sorts of oddities in one's possession. Regardless, that is part of a map detailing some of the route to the Book on the Isle."

Roni looked closer, her fingers tapping the edge of the table. Much of the map looked like many of the others she had seen in the Grand Library — one tunnel after another snaking through and looping around and looking no more organized than cooked spaghetti on a plate. But on this map, there was an open section with a small circular island in the middle. The words *Book on the Isle* had been printed neatly next to the circle.

"If you are willing," Kenneth said, leaning closer, "Yal-hara would like you to find the Book on the Isle and retrieve a kyolo stone. They are plentiful in the world that book leads to — you may be able to simply reach in and pluck one off the ground — and they are quite distinctive. With that stone, Yal-hara can create a simple compass that will lead her to a rift back into her universe."

Holding her breath, Roni reached out to touch the map. With so many gaps in what she had to work with, this fragment could be infinitely important. Certainly, Yal-hara believed it offered enough to guide her to this book — which suggested it would fill in a significant part of the overall mapping of the caverns. Unless, Roni held the same wishful thinking as Yal-hara. But before Roni could defeat her own hopes, she would have to take this paper to the map room in the Grand Library and see how well it fit in.

Holding the map in her hands, however, she paused. "Why is Yal-hara handling things this way? Why not come directly to the bookstore and talk with all of us? No matter what had happened in the past, Gram would help if —"

"Really? Have they helped you?"

"Me? I'm not stuck in somebody else's universe."

"You have Lost Time, don't you?"

Roni's muscles contracted. "How do you know —"

"It's not an unheard of phenomenon. From what I've been able to discern, nobody from any universe knows the exact cause — or causes, it may be more than one thing — but this kyolo stone might be able to help you, too. Perhaps it can lead you to some answers — ones you grandmother withholds from you. Just as she would withhold her aid to Yal-hara."

Folding the paper, Roni gave a short nod. A lump formed beneath her ribs and wormed its way into the pit of her stomach, but she placed the paper into her pocket. "I'll look into this," she said.

Kenneth's shoulder dropped an inch as he grinned. "Thank you." He rose from the table and slid his business card towards her. "Call me when you're ready." Straightening his coat, he walked away.

Roni sat motionless as she watched the strange man exit the diner. The torn piece of paper weighed down her coat. She took a deep breath — best not to raise her expectations.

Hard, though, when the man had mentioned her Lost Time. She had always thought that was a name Gram gave to her missing memories, but now it appeared to be something more — chalk it up to another lie from her grandmother. But since those lost memories revolved around the accident that stole her mother's life, Roni couldn't stop the excited questions racing through her mind — all centering around the promise of that piece of paper.

Her phone rang and she jumped. Glancing at the screen, she read — *Gram.*

As she swiped to accept the call, she placed her other hand under her thigh to stop its shaking. Nothing could be shaking — especially her voice. She had to make sure the Gram did not suspect anything out of the ordinary.

"H-Hello?" *Damn.*

But luck came her way. Gram was so wrapped up in her own purpose for calling that she made no reaction to Roni's nerves — or perhaps, she assumed Roni was nervous because of the call. It all reduced to Gram's two word reply. "You're late."

# CHAPTER 4

Although Olburg was not a huge town, it still took Roni twenty minutes to reach the bookstore. She burst in with a dismissive wave at Gram. "I know, I know. I'm here now."

Behind the counter, Gram crossed her arms underneath her large bosom. The scowl on her face deepened. "Are you wearing the same clothes as yesterday?"

Without slowing her pace, Roni said, "That depends — do you want me to go home and change or do you want me to get to work?"

In the aisle leading to the elevator, Roni weaved around a young woman. "Excuse me," the woman said, "I'm looking for —"

"Check with the woman up front, please."

"But —"

Smiling, Roni hopped into the elevator and closed the door. On her way down to the Grand Library, she patted her coat pocket, checking that the paper had not disappeared. Out of the elevator, she stepped into the main room and flicked on the lights.

She paused as the Library came to life. Despite all that she thought about being isolated from the Old Gang, she had to admit that she loved this place. Designed like the smoking room of an old estate, the main part of the Grand Library encompassed a far larger amount of space than such a room would require. When she took on the job of researcher for the Society, books had been stacked in dusty piles while papers were strewn about without much care. After a year of steady work, however, Roni had transformed most of the ill-used shelves into categorized, logical order. The wood gleamed, the light glittered, and the books had begun to discover their homes.

In addition to all the journals and diaries of the previous Parallel Society members, she had found numerous volumes of non-fiction written by Society members. Some of them were descriptions of how physics worked in different universes, some detailed the various powers different Society members had possessed throughout history, and some narrowed their focus to analyzing a specific location of the caverns or a single book chained to its walls. While all of these tomes excited the bookworm in Roni's head, she had come to love the room off to the right even more — the map room.

She had only started focusing on that room in the last four months. Her initial hope had been to take all the maps drawn by various expeditions and create a single, giant map of the caverns. But this proved far more challenging than she had expected. The maps were all different scales and styles. Many were fragments like the one in her pocket while others could not even be called a fragment. Some were nothing more than a rough sketch in a journal with barely a description of the surrounding area to orient the reader. In the end, Roni decided to create two versions of her Master Map — one on her computer and one on paper.

Taking all the completed, half-completed, and hardly-completed maps she had available, she used her computer to rescale everything to a uniform size. That took a long time until she got the hang of it. She then printed out the scaled-maps and went through the tedious job of figuring out how they connected. Like the early stages of tackling a complex jigsaw puzzle, she searched for the smallest connections between map pieces — especially anything that might resemble the ends. But after several tries, she realized she lacked key parts.

Roni stared at the map. Clenching the fragment, she searched for anything that it could connect with. Why give her the fragment if it couldn't be found? But with approximately half the wall covered in the paper maps and knowing that she had far more map than wall space, Roni had the sinking thought that this island holding a single book might be located far into the as-yet-unmapped portions of her project.

Except the fact that Kenneth Bay brought her the map fragment suggested the island would have to be near enough to reach; otherwise, it made a poor bribe for her help. Kenneth and Yal-hara had to know that Roni would use the fragment to locate the island — that's what they wanted her to do — so, it had to be in an accessible location.

Roni took the fragment over to her scanning table — an expense that bothered Gram but that she acquiesced to after Elliot and Sully defended the purchase. Upon scanning the fragment into the computer and having it rescale the image to match the rest, Roni started by letting the computer attempt to find where the fragment connected with the whole map. As expected, it came up empty. Well, it actually returned over four thousand results which pretty much meant the same thing. There were simply too many gaps in the overall map.

She then spent over an hour going through the four

thousand plus possibilities. Most were easily discarded, but some required several minutes of failed attempts to make the fragment fit. Even as she rotated and flipped the image on another attempt, part of her questioned if it would fit any of the map. The possibility existed that the fragment sat in the middle of a missing section with no connection to any of the current edges — like a puzzle piece for the center when all she had was the outer-frame.

Taking a break from the computer screen, Roni walked over to the map wall. Her eyes roved over the endless corridors and tunnels, the steps and drops, the widening spaces and narrowing fields. Somewhere in all of that mess, a single book sitting on a tiny island awaited her. She read off the names of the various spots that previous Society explorers had discovered and marked. Things like Stalactite Plains, Connor's Corner, the Cathedral, and Soft Slope — each name written by the hand of the cartographer, probably at the location itself.

Roni's mouth dropped open. She whirled back to the scanner and picked up the map fragment. There. In tiny script, neatly scrawled on the bottom edge — the name Gerald Waterfield.

She hurried back to the main room and brought up the library catalog on her computer. Typing in *Gerald Waterfield*, her fingers tingled and her lips lifted at the corners. But no results came from her search. That didn't mean anything yet — Roni had only digitized the Library holdings she had placed on the shelves. She had years of work ahead of her before the whole library could be searched via computer.

In the back corner of the main room, the old card catalog gathered dust. Much of it no longer corresponded with the actual locations of books, but for the moment, Roni only wanted to confirm the book's existence. After a short rifling through a drawer of typed and hand-written index cards, she found it:

> *Waterfield, Gerald. The Journal of Gerald Waterfield. incl 4 maps and 7 plates. Society member 1807-1842. Loc: Row 21, WAT*

Roni snagged the card out of the drawer and worked her way through the Library. Many of the shelves had been moved throughout the years. She had moved several herself. But she doubted many would have shifted the books far from where they had been shelved.

As she walked up and down several aisles, she wondered at the immense effort required to move the entire operation from Paris to England to America. All those books in the caverns chained to the walls — where were they held in England? How did Grace Covington, the leader of the Society at the time, even know about the caverns in Pennsylvania? And with Gram, Elliot, and Sully nearing the ends of their lives, did that mean that Roni would someday be responsible for moving everything again? She thought over the map and all its missing parts. Moving all the books in those caverns without an accident destroying universes would be impossible.

At the end of one aisle, Roni found ten stacks of dust-covered books piled as high as her chest. On the wall, small gold plates marked the old row numbers — 19, 20, and 21. She walked back to her work desk and dragged her chair to the ten piles of books.

Though she wanted to rifle through it all to find Waterfield's journal, part of her could not resist organizing the books into ready-to-go piles that she could come back to later. Despite the extra time, she managed to get through three-quarters of the books in under an hour — getting distracted only when she came upon a book with Grace

Covington's name on it. Turned out to be a biography rather than a personal journal. She set that book to one side and continued on.

And then she found it. A leather bound journal that smelled of long years outdoors by a campfire. The pages crackled, instantly bringing images of a hard-faced man of good upbringing, exploring the underside of the world, aware that he did his part to save so many lives and that so few would ever read his words or know his contribution. Roni clutched the journal against her chest like a schoolgirl in an old film.

Returning to her desk with the book and her chair, she settled in, intent on approaching her find carefully. While the pages were stiff, they did not break under her touch. Good. She had no desire to bring the journal upstairs to the floor where Elliot and Sully repaired old volumes of all kinds.

Before she read a single word, she sifted through page after page. Waterfield's sharp-angled script and messy use of ink would be difficult to decipher, but she had read enough journals from further back than the 19th century — she could handle this one. Searching deeper into the book, she finally found the key page she sought — the torn page displaying the rest of Waterfield's map. To be sure, she retrieved the fragment and matched it up with the journal. A perfect fit.

Picking up the journal to get the rest of the map scanned into the computer, a yellowed card fell from the back of the book, flipping to the ground like a fallen leaf. The library checkout card. As she picked it up, she made a mental note that the checkout system would have to be digitized as well. Setting the card into the sleeve on the journal's back page, her heart jumped.

The last person to check out the book — *Elliot Kenmana.*

# CHAPTER 5

For several minutes, Roni stood immobile in the middle of the library, the old checkout card held tight between her fingers. Her mind blanked. She kept seeing the clean, steady penmanship that men rarely possessed. She only knew one man who wrote like that — Elliot, of course.

Closing her eyes, she tried to think straight. First, she needed to confirm that this wasn't a coincidence. Perhaps there had been another Elliot Kenwana with excellent penmanship. She didn't believe it, but going through the thought process provided her body and brain with an action. She walked over to several book piles throughout the room and randomly opened books. None had been checked out by Elliot. While that did not prove anything concrete, it did suggest that he was connected to all of this — whatever *this* was. After all, if he had simply been a curious reader, she would have found other titles he had explored. That would have made her feel better. She inspected more of the books, but after twenty minutes without finding Elliot's name, she decided that would be confirmation enough.

Resisting the urge to race upstairs and confront the old

man, Roni walked the journal over to the map room. As the new map fragment scanned into the computer, she reorganized her thoughts. It would do her no good to approach Elliot without more information. She had to attack this problem like a police detective. Whenever possible, a detective interrogated a suspect with enough knowledge of the truth that they had a good shot of catching a lie. Roni knew so little at the moment that, no matter what Elliot said, she would never be able to separate fact from fiction.

*Why am I assuming that he'd lie to me?* That thought troubled her. Gram would lie. Gram had lied. But Elliot? She always thought of him as the most honest man in her life.

After the scan completed, Roni once more sent the image through the computer program to find matches to the existing map. Only 2900 results this time. Better than before. But over the next few hours, she ended up in the same place. The fragment did not connect with any part of the map.

The grandfather clock standing against a support pillar chimed six o'clock, and Roni's stomach rumbled on cue. Arching her head back, she smacked the arm of her chair. The entire day had gone, and she had made so little progress. The island in the lake could be practically anywhere in the caverns, and she had come across nothing that pointed to why Elliot would have an interest in any of this.

Except for Yal-hara. If Roni could believe even part of what Kenneth Bay had said, then at one time, Yal-hara asked the Old Gang for help and they refused her. Except that didn't make much sense. Roni couldn't see Elliot turning away any living creature.

Which left Roni with a baffled mind, an empty stomach,

and a need for answers. No point in stalling further — her claims at a detective's approach sounded good, but she knew better. No secret evidence would be revealed unless she started kicking over stones. She had to deal with Elliot.

Stepping out of the elevator onto the main floor, Roni planned on inviting Elliot to dinner. A nice, public place would keep their conversation calm — not that she thought Elliot would raise his voice, but as a precaution against whatever secret lay beneath. Plus, she needed to eat. But when she walked toward the big table in the center of the room, she found Elliot, Sully, and Gram all dressed nicely and ready to leave.

"What's the occasion?" she asked.

Gram flipped open her compact to check on her hair. "Nothing at all. For many years now, we've made sure to get together for a nice dinner at least once every month. It's a good way to keep our team strong and our morale up."

Placing a tweed hat on his head, Sully said, "Oh, we've made a mistake. You should've been asked to join us. How could we do such a thing? You're part of the team now."

Elliot gave Sully a squeeze on the shoulder. "You are absolutely right. Please, Roni, accept our apology. We did not intend to exclude you. Rather, we have been doing this dinner for so long that we all simply got ready to go without thinking about it. It is our old habit."

Snapping the compact shut, Gram said, "Boys, don't pressure her. I'm sure she has a million things more fun to do than spend an evening stuck with three old folks like us." She looked at Roni. "Of course, dear, if you'd like to join us, you're more than welcome."

Roni could not read her face. Did she want Roni to join or not? A piece of Roni broke inside — how had things devolved so far between them that she would even question if Gram wanted her around? Worse than that, Roni knew exactly when this change began — a year ago, on the night she first learned of Gram's powers, the caverns, and the Society. Once the Old Gang's secret had been revealed, much of the warmth and stern caring that made up Gram's foundation disappeared.

"Maybe next time," Roni said. "It's been a long day."

Gram raised an eyebrow but said nothing more. As the Old Gang left the bookstore, Roni thought she had made the right choice. She didn't want to be sitting through a long meal while itching to speak with Elliot privately, and she didn't want to talk about Waterfield's journal with Gram and Sully until she had more information at hand. Besides, Roni was the New Gang — a gang of one for the moment, but the New Gang nonetheless. She would be better off getting comfortable with that fact.

Having the bookstore to herself, she ordered a cheesesteak, retrieved the Waterfield journal from the Grand Library, and settled at the big table in the main room. Reading while eating, surrounded by the quiet of the closed store and the blanketing aroma of old books, she allowed herself to relax — not entirely, but enough.

The journal had many entries covering a wide variety of topics, but she found three key details within Waterfield's words. The first had nothing to do with Yal-hara nor Elliot's possible involvement. Rather it focused on the nature of the caves themselves —

> *I must admit that I have pondered these caverns at great length. The rest of the team seems accepting of the structure and shows no more curiosity, but I find that infuriating to say the least. I requested the opportunity to perform certain experiments upon the cavern walls to determine how it can be that I find references to these very caverns within the diaries of*

*Society members from over a hundred years past. This is simply impossible when one considers the verifiable fact that the Society has changed locations throughout the world on numerous occasions. How can it be that we all utilize the same caverns?*

Roni jotted down a note, marking where she could find this entry again at a later time. But as she read on, she could not stop her own curiosity —

*I've been denied my request. Short-sightedness appears to be the common ground for my peers. They fear that interfering with the cavern walls might cause damage to our purpose. Since we do not understand the cavern itself, they reason that we cannot comprehend how our actions upon it might behave. But is not that the very point of experimentation? How are we to learn if not by trial?*

*Well, it has become apparent that I have another resource for information. The Grand Library has several volumes by Mr. Augustus Kincaid who grappled with the same concerns. According to the good gentleman, the caverns must exist within a universe of their own. It is that simple. When we step through the entrance into the caverns, we leave our universe and walk through to another. The caverns universe, therefore, is the storage container for all the breaches we investigate and attempt to close. Fascinating as a hypothesis, but one that requires deeper attention to prove valid or false. Of course, I shall never divulge to my teammates that there is this information. They would argue that*

*such      information      makes      experimentation
unrequired.*

Roni wrote down the name Augustus Kincaid to deal
with another day. The next entry she found useful had been
written one page before the map Waterfield had drawn. He
described a seven day journey through the caverns which
ended with the discovery of a narrow river. He named it for
himself — Waterfield River. None of his teammates joined
him on the expedition, so he chose to return before
traveling the river. A month later, despite his teammates
refusal to help, he found his way back to the river. This
time he brought supplies to build a simple raft and took to
the water.

Roni then read:

> *The waters of my namesake carried me through
> tunnels upon which no other path could be taken,
> and following a rather unsettling patch of rough
> currents, I was deposited into a massive lake with a
> lone island in the center.*

With her hands shaking from adrenaline, Roni could
barely write her notes. No wonder the map never matched
up with anything she had already scanned through — it
never would. The access to the lake involved a river, not a
path. Clearly, Waterfield found a route back because he
lived to complete his journal and shelve it in the Grand
Library — *and why couldn't that route be used to get there?* — but
for the moment, Roni reveled in the idea that all she needed
to do was find the river.

The last entry she read that made a strong impression
came only pages later. Waterfield navigated his raft to the
island — *"a circular clump of empty sand no bigger than the parlor*

*room of a home."* Almost empty. In the center, a stone pedestal had been built. Sitting on the pedestal, Waterfield found the Book of the Isle — a single volume chained to the stone.

He wrote:

> *I cannot account for the sensations that overcame me, the thoughts that grew within my mind, but I had the undeniable urge to open that book. What kind of universe would be so special that it received an island all to itself? Quite naturally, I considered the possibility that the book accessed a most dangerous universe, one that should never be opened. And yet, my heart denied this. I could feel a loving embrace, a warmth of welcome that no evil could ever produce. Since it was my instincts that brought me to this place, despite the disagreements with my fellow Society members, I chose to adhere to my instincts once more. I opened the book.*

> *I discovered Heaven.*

The front door rattled as Gram unlocked it, and the Old Gang bumbled inside. Roni closed the journal and grabbed her notes, but Sully had already stumbled further in.

"You had quite a bit to drink," she said with a lighthearted chuckle. She slid the book into her bag, but Sully's brow knitted downward.

"Whatcha reading there?" He burped and pointed at the bag.

"Nothing important."

"Don't be like that. It's good to be a reader. I've always loved that about you. And you've got strong taste. Good taste."

Elliot stepped over and steadied Sully. "You have had too much to drink. Leave Roni alone."

"Since you won't drink, I gotta do it for both of us."

Gram laughed. "You didn't have to do it for me, but you did anyway."

Roni shouldered her bag. "Well, you all need to get some sleep. I'll see you in the morning."

As she walked by Sully, however, he dipped his hand into her bag and pulled out the journal. "Well, well, let's see here. *The Journal of Gerald Waterfield.* Who the heck is that?"

Roni spun back and snatched the journal — but not in time. Elliot had frozen. He stared at Roni, his eyes glistening as his jaw shivered.

# CHAPTER 6

Holding onto the table for balance, Sully waved his hand in the air. "What's with you two? Somebody tell me who Gerald Whatever-his-name-is is?"

From behind, Roni heard the hardline tones of Gram upset. "He's the man who discovered the Book on the Isle."

The words sobered Sully fast. "Oh. Isn't that where Elliot ... oh, I see." He looked to Roni and shook his head. "You shouldn't have done that."

"Done what?" Roni said, her focus still on Elliot. "What is this island to you?"

Elliot brushed a tear before it could fall. He glanced upward, perhaps gaining strength from above, and opened his mouth to respond. But Gram stepped between them.

"We will not be discussing that island," she said. "Elliot, help Sully get upstairs before the poor man can't stand anymore." With a meek nod, Elliot did as instructed. Gram then turned to Roni. "You need to forget about the Book on the Isle. You need to forget about Waterfield and anything you read in his journal. The man was a crackpot, and his writings have done more harm to members of the

Parallel Society than any other journal in our library."

Roni's blood heated fast. "Another secret. I suppose I should get a list of books that I'm banned from reading. It'll make it easier for you to hide things from me."

"You should know better than to question me about things you aren't informed on."

"How can I be informed when you won't tell me anything? You want to keep me trapped downstairs, but you are being pigheaded to think that you're protecting me. Not after a year of knowing the truth about our world. If anything, you put my life in greater danger. How am I supposed to make informed decisions, to lead the next group of the Society, when I know so little? I guess I'll have to do like Waterfield and explore the caverns myself."

Gram slammed her purse on the table. "You will not. To do so is to risk death, and I won't have it. Whatever your problems with me, they do not give you the right to break ranks, to go off on your own, make your own choices with any of this."

"You don't get to tell me —"

"I damn well do. Being the leader of this group says so. If you defy me, there will be serious repercussions."

Roni's face dropped. "Are you really threatening me? What was the point of taking me in after Mom's death, of raising me to be strong and independent, if you're going to treat me like this?"

"The fact that you ask such a question, once again shows me that you are not ready for the greater responsibilities of the Society. We cannot be selfish. We cannot go off on our own like Gerald Waterfield and ignore the others of the team. To do so invites disaster. And any disaster involving the Society can mean disaster for all of mankind."

"Then why not work with me instead of against me?"

"You sound just like Waterfield. You're happy to cooperate as long as we all go along with you. Well, that's not the way this works."

"But —"

"That's it. This is done. No more talk about Waterfield or the Book on the Isle. I don't want you mentioning journeys into the caverns because there won't be any. And above all else, you do not speak a word of any of this to Elliot. The poor man has suffered enough. Now, go home before I really get mad."

Roni saw the cold fury in Gram's face. There would be no reasoning with her that night. But Roni did not want to be reasonable. With a huff, she stormed across the room, flung open the front door, and stomped out.

The frosty night air slammed into her with a strong wind. Hugging her arms against the chill, she trudged along the sidewalk. Her thoughts raged.

Gram had no right to impose her will upon them. Being the leader did not make her a dictator. Worse, she acted like she knew everything, had all the answers, but if that were true, then she abandoned Yal-hara purposefully. And what purpose could warrant trapping a being in our universe when it doesn't belong here?

Oh, that old woman had so many secrets held close to the vest — and she dared to criticize Roni for being selfish!

Roni walked onward and tried to calm her anger. She thought about the cavern with all those books leading to all those universes. Each streetlight she passed under, each flicker of television or computer screen in a window, each car driving by with its headlights flashing over her — all the lights like universes spread out before her. And all she needed to do was find one small light sitting on an island.

But then she thought of Elliot and the horror on his face when he saw the journal. As much as Roni wanted to

ignore all Gram had said, her final words about Elliot
echoed — *the poor man has suffered enough.* Roni wanted to ask
him, but she had dredged up something dark, and she
couldn't do that to him. At least, not unless she had no
other choice.

*And I do have a choice.*

She had Waterfield's journal, after all. He had made the
trip to the Isle by himself. So could she.

Except she didn't want to. She did not have the gene for
becoming an explorer, mounting expeditions into
uncharted territories. The only reason she looked into any
of this was Yal-hara. It was a moral choice, not one of
discovery, not one of defiance.

*No,* she thought as she glanced back toward the
bookstore. The moral aspect of it — helping Yal-hara find
her way home — was only one part. Mostly, she wanted to
get the kyolo stones to help her with her lost memories.

Perhaps, then, she was selfish. But before she attempted
to traverse the caverns alone, before she took steps against
Gram's wishes that could never be taken back, before she
gambled everything, she figured she should at least try her
only other source of information one last time. It had been
years since she really tried to talk to him, to do anything
more than sit by his side, to attempt to get through. Yet it
seemed like the right thing to do.

Nodding in the chilly air, seeing her breath plume out in
vanishing vapor, she thought, *Okay then. Tomorrow morning,
I'm going to visit my father.*


The Belmont Behavioral Hospital had been constructed in
West Philadelphia, and if not for a small sign out front,
there would be no way to know the building's purpose. But
Roni knew. Whenever she drove this way to visit her father,

whenever she passed beneath the gates and parked in the visitor section, whenever she heard the echoing click of her shoes or smelled the hospital aroma of disinfectant blended with disease, she could not avoid remembering why this building existed.

"Ms. Rider, good to see you again," the front desk nurse said.

"Uh-huh." Roni didn't mean to be rude, but visiting her father never settled well within her. She had no room for small talk.

The nurse handed over a clipboard and plastered on a smile. Roni knew the routine. Sign in, wait to be called, then get escorted to the visiting room where she would sit and wait for somebody to bring her father out. Meanwhile, other visitors spoke in low voices with their loved ones. Some of the patients responded. Others gazed off half-dead. For Roni, it was always a coin-toss which version of her father would appear.

An orderly opened the doors, wheeled Mr. Rider into the visitor's room, and stopped at Roni's table. "Your father's been doing real well lately. I'm sure he's excited to see you today." The orderly patted Mr. Rider's shoulder and walked off.

Growing up, Roni's image of her father centered on his shoulders — big, broad shoulders that she could sit on at a parade or when she was tired of walking. Muscular shoulders that never weakened no matter how many times she asked to be swung through the air. The shoulders of a powerful bear.

But seeing him now, she shuddered. All the strength had left him. His arms, once thick enough for Roni to do chin-ups on, had become thin reeds. His eyes sank into his skeletal head. Worse, she saw no light behind them, no spark of cognizance.

Yet she had to try. "Hi, Dad. It's Roni. You been doing okay?"

No response.

"Things for me have been unusual. I mean, a year ago my biggest problem was that I had no direction in life. Remember that? Gram always bickering that I needed to pick a career already." Roni snickered. "I was so stressed out about all that, but I'm telling you, that was easy street. Now, the fate of the universe depends on me."

His mouth dropped open an inch. Odd. But Roni figured it was nothing more than his drugs kicking in.

"Anyway, I'm sorry I haven't been here more often. I suppose you get it. Not like you signed yourself in here because you thought you were spending too much time with me. I mean, let's be honest. After mom died, you fell apart and you couldn't be bothered with me. Oh, don't worry. I don't hold it against you. Really. I did at one time, but I'm all grown up now. And ever since my life has changed, this last year, well, my perspective on a lot of things has changed, too. After all, nobody is what they seem on the outside. I grew up thinking Gram and Elliot and Sully were the cutest, little old trio. Never would I have guessed they were heroes. They really are. Call themselves The Parallel Society."

His head turned towards her. His eyes focused on her.

Roni tried to speak more, but her throat constricted. Nodding and smiling like an eager child, she finally found her words. "It's true. You know about it? The three of them go around closing up rifts with other universes. Strange, though, that they always talk about it in those terms — universes — when really they only fix things on Earth. I wonder if there are rifts billions of miles away from here. There must be. Maybe there's another Society on another planet out there."

He shifted in his wheelchair an inch, leaning closer as she spoke.

"You understand what I'm talking about, don't you? You do. I can see it. Now that I'm thinking about it, I shouldn't be surprised. They offered a job to Mom. She turned it down, of course, but no matter how wild a life she led, she always came back to you. So, she probably told you about Gram. Did you ever learn about the caverns? You'd be amazed to see them."

His hand reached out and found her wrist. Though his grip shook, she could tell that if he had more strength, he would have held her tight. In a whisper, he said, "Stay away from the caverns."

"Dad? You hear me?"

With more force, he said, "Stay away from the dark thing in the caverns."

"I'm not in the caverns. Not regularly. I'm just a researcher. You don't have to worry. I'll never see the dark thing."

Tears brimmed on the edges of his eyes. "The dark thing — the hellspider — it will destroy you."

Roni's muscles froze. "What?"

His head drooped as his eyes rolled.

"No," Roni said. "Come on. Tell me."

"The hellspider," he said in a slow drone. "Leave it alone." Then his eyes closed and he snored.

Roni stayed for twenty minutes more, trying to bring her father back. Twice he lifted his head and looked about the room, but he never regained lucidity that day. Eventually, the orderlies wheeled him off to his bed.


Driving to Olburg, Roni tried to make sense of everything he had said. Except none of the parts appeared to connect with the bits of information she had acquired. Even if there had been a connection, it might have been nothing more than lunatic ravings. *A hellspider?* She couldn't fully trust anything he said. Yet she couldn't dismiss it either.

Not that it mattered. Gram now knew about some of it — enough that she had shut down the whole thing. Roni had built up an idea that she would present all her research to the team, that she would then explain about Kenneth Bay and Yal-hara, and that Gram would be so impressed, she would insist on Roni leading the charge into the caverns. That would never happen now.

"Damn it," she yelled in her car. Turning on the radio, she blasted classic rock for a few miles but flicked it off before the first song had ended. That was her career in the Society. Over before it began. Not even a one-hit wonder.

She found a parking space on the street several blocks from her apartment. As she strolled home, she tried to let go of the failure and stress. If she could accept her position as the librarian and not the adventurer, she would do far better. And why not? She never wanted to go into the caverns in the first place. Never wanted any of it. Why not simply hole up in the Grand Library? She could be of great assistance to those equipped to deal with the other universes, yet she should never have to bloody her hands.

Chuckling, she picked up her pace. That sounded good except for the part where she would have to be under the thumb of Gram. Plus, one day, Gram would find somebody to take over — not Roni, of course, because the researcher can't be the leader — which would leave Roni being under the thumb of yet another formidable Society member. No, that wouldn't work either.

"Finally, you are home," a voice called out.

Roni looked up and all she saw ahead of her was trouble. Elliot waited for her in the doorway.

# CHAPTER 7

As Roni opened the door to her apartment, Elliot brushed through straight for the center of the room. With his cane, he pushed aside the robe and dirty blouse discarded on the floor. Standing between her old television and her worn couch, he lifted the cane shoulder-height with his right hand. His left traced a figure eight repeatedly.

Roni knew not to speak while Elliot cast a spell. She gently closed the door before going down the hall to the bathroom. When she returned a few minutes later, the air around Elliot's hand shimmered. She leaned against the wall and waited.

The shimmering increased its frequency right before Roni heard a pop. Then her ears clogged up as if from the pressure of sitting in an airplane changing altitude. Rubbing her ears, she tried to get them to clear, but nothing helped.

Lowering his hands, Elliot turned towards her. Despite all the sounds around her being muted, when he spoke, his voice cut through the thick gauze in the air. "This spell will not last long, so I advise you to be honest with me. For the moment, nobody can hear what we say. Anyone attempting to snoop on us will know nothing."

"Who would be snooping?" Roni asked, her own voice louder than she expected.

"Not everybody in the world that knows the truth agrees with the Society. We have our enemies."

Roni wondered where Yal-hara and Kenneth Bay fell in that dichotomy — friend or foe. She had accepted them at face value — mostly because of the map fragment — but seeing the deep concern in Elliot's eyes worried her.

Placing both his hands on the top of his cane, Elliot tilted forward. "Now is the time when you must tell me all that you know about the Book on the Isle and how you came to know it."

"I just stumbled upon it. I was working in the Grand Library like always, and I came across Waterfield's journal. You were the last to check it out, so I got curious."

Elliot shook his head. "Even without powers I can see that you are lying. I have known you since you were little, after all. Do not try to deceive me. I shall offer you one more opportunity. Tell me the truth." His stern expression cracked for an instant, and beneath it, Roni saw mournful sadness.

"I'm sorry," she said. "Here's the truth." And she told him everything that had occurred since Kenneth Bay sat down across from her in the Olburg Chestnut.

When she finished, Elliot gave a thoughtful grunt. "Yal-hara. We never did the right thing with her. We wanted to, but there was no way to pinpoint her specific universe. Not that we know."

"Why couldn't you just open the book that captured the original rift? Let her go through."

"Because we never did capture it. It disappeared on its own as if that universe merely grazed ours instead of intersecting it."

"Yal-hara says she needs this kyolo stone to find another

rift to her universe. That with the stone, she can find her way home. Is that right? Is she telling me the truth?"

"Maybe."

"But these stones are everywhere in the Book on the Isle. She said that. Is that much true?"

"It once was true, but I have not been to that place in many years."

Roni pushed off the wall, her head cocked in disbelief. "You've been there? You've seen the Book on the Isle?"

Closing his eyes as if the words might cause him to scream, he opted instead to nod.

A dark thought struck her. "What's the hellspider?"

Elliot's eyes snapped open. "Hellspider? I have never heard of that."

"I thought we were going to be honest here."

"I am. I have never heard of nor have I ever seen something called a hellspider."

She believed him. "What about my Lost Time? Yal-hara said that the stones she wants could also help me with my memory."

"I don't know."

"How can you know so little about this when it's obvious that you're connected to it all?"

"Because I have never met Yal-hara, so I cannot confirm the truth of her words. I am assuming that you also have not met her."

Crossing her arms, Roni said, "Just her guy, Kenneth Bay. He called himself her emissary."

"I know him. His father, Roger Bay, was the man I dealt with on the few occasions Yal-hara reached out to us."

"If you worked with them before, then you should know whether I can trust them."

He chuckled. "You most certainly cannot trust them. But that does not mean they have lied to you. Yal-hara has been stuck here for a long time, and she wants to find her way back to her world. That much is true. Whether the kyolo stones can save her, whether they can help you, I do not know. I doubt Yal-hara knows for sure, either."

"So this is all a gamble?"

"Perhaps a better way to say this would be that Yal-hara is making a highly educated guess."

Roni walked to the couch and slumped into its lumpy cushions. "Then I have to try, right? I have to go to this Book on the Isle and get some of those kyolo stones. And I have to prepare myself for the fact that it might not work — at least, not for me."

"The Book on the Isle leads to a wondrous place."

"Waterfield wrote that it's a paradise."

"Indeed, it is. Possibly the most extraordinary world I've ever seen. Yet such worlds of beauty and peace can do more harm than the dark, evil worlds." Elliot's gaze lowered. "A world of paradise gives hope. And hope — real, pure hope — is destined to be destroyed."

"Maybe," she said, a dread excitement building as a bonfire grows from a single flame. "But knowing the place is real, confirming it because you've been there, that sort of means I have to go now. I can't turn away. I have to try — for Yal-hara and for myself."

Roni heard a high-pitched whine followed by a pop similar to the one earlier. Elliot shuffled toward the front door. "The spell is done," he said.

"Thank you for telling me this. It's going to help me make this decision."

"Do not lie to yourself. You have already made that decision."

"I suppose I did. That's it then. I'm going to the Isle."

"Good. I assumed as much when you first mentioned the Isle. That is why I have taken the liberty of packing supplies for the trip. We should get started right away."

"We?"

"I expect you to come along. It would be too lonely to do it by myself. Now, get some clothes together and we will be off."

Roni grinned. "Shouldn't we sleep on it? I mean, I could use some rest before hiking into a cavern for days."

"The longer we wait, the more likely that Gram and Sully will attempt to stop us. Who do you think I was casting that spell against?"

"The spell is over. Shouldn't you be quiet about it now?"

Elliot blushed. "I am old. I forget things. Maybe I am also too paranoid. But Gram has strong feelings about this subject, and she will not want me going to the Isle. So, we must be on our way. If you are too tired, we will find a place to rest once we are out of Gram's reach. Okay? Good. Now, let us begin."

# CHAPTER 8

An hour later, Roni walked down the stairs from the main floor of the bookstore into the basement. The Grand Library was further below ground, but this low-ceiling, musty area filled with boxes of old periodicals and dusty dictionaries led to the door with the medieval padlock — Gram's private office. Normally, the door remained closed and locked, but Elliot had already used a spell to "pick" the lock.

The last time Roni entered this room without permission, she discovered the caverns and her whole worldview shifted beneath her feet. She had been terrified to go in there. This time, however, she went in willingly — with a purpose.

Fluorescent lights hung from a tiled ceiling which only added to the utilitarian style of the room. Like an old 1970s cop show, the room appeared to be a metal box with metal shelves for the numerous books Gram collected. But unlike any room elsewhere in the world, a large hole in the back wall opened into a cavern.

Elliot stood by this hole. He wore a long winter coat and a tweed, newsboy cap. Roni shouldered a backpack as she approached.

"All set," she said. She had clothes for three days and a folder with hardcopy printouts of the maps. "There are missing chunks," she said. "The maps will only help us so far."

With a grandfatherly smile, Elliot tapped the side of his head. "This still works. I shall get us to the river, and the river will get us to the Isle."

"Just in case, I also brought this," she said, pulling out Waterfield's journal. "I haven't had the chance to read it thoroughly, but I'm guessing there's more in here to help us."

Bringing such an old and irreplaceable text should have caused her deep worry — it was risky, to say the least — but nothing could be more essential than the words of a man who had already made the journey. Such vital information far outweighed her concerns over possible damage done to the journal.

"Yes," Elliot said. "That is a good backup, in case something happens to me."

Roni didn't like his tone, but she let it pass. Elliot stepped forward, and Roni glimpsed the cart behind him — a wagon with a metal rod to pull it, wooden crate sides, and four rugged wheels. Inside, she saw jugs of water, boxes of food, camping gear, and clothes. An uncomfortable sensation crawled across her skin.

"Wow," she muttered. "I never thought to bring any of that stuff."

He snickered. "Don't feel bad. My first trip into the caverns, I didn't even have the sense to bring a change of clothes. We were only going to fetch an empty book from a specific spot, and we only planned to be gone a few hours. But I fell, slid down a muddy incline and splashed into a puddle the size of this room. The water was cold and the air cool, and there was no easy way back up. Gram and Sully had to carefully climb down, which took a half-hour, and then we had to walk far out of our way to get back to where we were originally — which required most of the day. I could not do so sopping wet. So, I striped down and proceeded for several hours in the nude."

Roni laughed. "I'm sure Sully never let you live that down."

"Nor your grandmother. She kept threatening to take my picture."

"I can't imagine that, but I'll take your word for it." With a shrug, she added, "I guess that's all we need. Let's go."

"One more thing." Elliot reached into his wagon and pulled out a leather-bound journal. "A proper researcher will document her experiences."

Roni kept her eyes on the journal in case she cried. She accepted the gift as a priceless heirloom. Passing her hand across the top, she noticed the silk ribbon used to mark her place and smelled the rich aroma of the pages. Holding the journal at her side, she stepped in close and hugged Elliot with her free arm.

"Thank you," she said.

"I can think of no greater honor than to take this first big step with you. Now, let us begin."

Before Roni heard Gram's voice, she heard Gram's footsteps. Turning towards the doorway, she saw the familiar scowl. She could feel everything falling apart.

Gram gripped the cross around her neck. "I don't know which of you two to be more angry with. At least Roni's been consistently defiant from the start. But you. How could you go behind my back like this?"

"I am not behind your back," Elliot said, his tone more forceful than Roni had expected.

"Really? So, it was merely coincidence that you cast a dampening spell when you went to my granddaughter's apartment."

"Not at all. I wanted our conversation to be private. Leading this group does not give you the right to know all that we think, feel, and do. It most certainly does not give you the right to spy on us."

Caught between two angry old people, Roni scooted out of the way.

Though Gram had to lift her chin in order to meet Elliot's eyes, she seemed the larger of the two. "I was looking out for the safety of my granddaughter and you, for that matter. But everybody is hellbent on doing whatever they want. That won't work. We have to be united or we will lose any battle we encounter."

"I agree. Yet you seem to consider the word *united* to mean that we follow your rules at all times."

Roni cringed, bracing for the tirade Gram would unleash. But instead, Gram stepped back with a disappointed grin. She glanced at Roni. "I didn't want to believe him, but Sully told me that you saw things this way. And now I hear it from my own teammate, too." To Elliot, she added, "Do you really think of me as a dictator? Come now, you know me better than that. I admit I am strong-willed, but I have a duty to maintain the strength of this group, the safety of us, as well as that of the entire universe."

Elliot placed his hand on her shoulder. "That duty belongs to us all. Whether she knows it or not, I am sure that Roni would be taking this journey alone, if necessary. I would not let that happen."

To Roni's further surprise, Gram's chin trembled. "But she wants to go to the Isle."

"I know."

"Are you sure you're ready to face them?"

"I have hid for too long." Elliot glanced back at the opening to the caverns. "And for Roni, this is not about my past."

"Oh?"

Roni stepped in front of Elliot. "This about Yal-hara."

Gram laced her fingers as her face darkened. "I see. You're after the kyolo stones."

"You know about them?"

"It's a myth. Yal-hara is old and desperate for anything that'll get her home."

Roni looked toward the caverns. "I'm still going. I'll find out for myself if it's a myth."

Gram opened her arm toward Roni. "Then we all go — together." Roni stared at her grandmother, trying to piece together what had happened. "Come on," Gram said. "I expect a hug."

Rushing over, Roni wrapped her arms around Gram. "You're really okay with this?"

"Not at all. But this is clearly something the two of you need to do, and I will not sit upstairs while you both risk your lives."

"But there's nothing —"

"Oh Lord, my dear, you must learn this right away — any trip into the caverns is a risk to your life. Any single step in there must be treated with cautiousness and respect for danger. Understand?"

She nodded. "I will."

"Good. Then I have only one question." Gram pointed at Elliot's cart. "What the heck is that?"

Elliot knocked his cane against the cart's tires. "What? It is strong and easy to pull. You do not expect me to carry all of these items."

"That thing won't last one day in the caverns. Once you

get beyond the well-worn paths, there's rugged terrain and muddy areas — you know all about those. I would be shocked if those tires didn't pop flat within a few hours. And also —"

"Okay, okay. What do you suggest?"

"Sully, of course."

Roni laughed. "Sully's going to carry all of this?"

"No, not directly. But the moment I realized what Elliot was up to, I got Sully working." She cocked her head toward the door. "Sully? You coming?"

From further in the basement, Sully's voice rang out. "You people are so impatient. I'll be there in a second."

A moment later, he walked into the room. Behind him, on a rope, he brought in a full-sized donkey-golem made of clay. It had a broad, flat back and thick legs. Its head lacked a mouth but it did have eyes. Somewhere in its clay body, Sully had written Hebrew words on a slip of paper — a spell to create life from a non-living thing. He would have slipped the paper into the donkey form, whispered an incantation into its ear, and the donkey-golem would spring to life.

"One of these days," Sully said, huffing as he walked, "you will give me more than a few hours' notice and I'll be able to create a beautiful creature instead of a mere semblance like this."

"As long as it can haul our gear, I don't care if it only has half of a head."

Patting the donkey-golem's flank, Sully said to it, "Don't listen to that old crab. You're more than labor to us. We appreciate all the hard work you're about to do."

Gram stepped in front of Roni and Elliot. "Come on, now. Quit gawking and help load her up."

Although nothing that had happened went along with Roni's expectations, part of her warmed at the idea of Elliot and Sully joining her. Even Gram's presence gave Roni a small sense of comfort. The Old Gang knew the way to the Isle, and they knew the dangers to be found in the caverns. At least, she hoped they knew.

When they finished packing one section of the donkey-golem, Gram made a motion with her wrist. A thin, metal chain flew out of her sleeve. The chain wrapped itself around the gear, securing it to the donkey-golem.

After they had finished transferring all of the supplies, Gram gestured towards Elliot. "Last chance. You really want to do this?"

"It is long overdue."

Gram gazed back over the team. She seemed to be weighing this final decision in her head. At length, and without further word, she led the way into the caverns. Elliot followed and Sully came up with his donkey-golem nudging along.

Roni stopped at the edge. She had done this before, yet it felt new. This was her first foray into the caverns as a member of the Parallel Society. This was her first time setting foot in the caverns having read that it existed in another universe. Whatever they encountered in there would become part of Society history. The idea filled her with a sense of importance — and dread.

Swallowing down her rising dark thoughts, she entered the caverns.

# CHAPTER 9

For the first half hour, Roni could not have been more awed. Once they traveled beyond the small portion she had experienced a year ago, the caverns treated her with one astonishing view after another. Enormous ceilings with thousands of stalactites — sharp like teeth. Books leading to other universes hung on chains, dangling in the air like muted wind chimes. Winding paths spiraled off into the dark, and narrow crevices had been worn smooth like glass.

In every direction, no matter how high up or how far away, Roni saw books. Endless books. Each one chained to the walls, chained to themselves, or lined up behind tightly wound chains. Some books occupied huge sections of wall by themselves while others had been crowded together, shoved into tiny spaces, locked away like prisoners. Each book opened to a rift into another universe. Hundreds of years of the Parallel Society capturing these rifts, putting them in these magic books, and housing them in these caverns. It looked full, yet Roni had seen the maps — there was room for hundreds of thousands more. Maybe millions.

The cavern air maintained a steady coolness — warmer

than the autumn air outside in Olburg but chilly nonetheless. It smelled fresh, too. As if all the moss of a forest had found its way into the stone surrounding them.

Lighting from various decades had been strung along the pathway revealing the history of those who came before like striation patterns. Modern, small rectangles that cast enormous bright, pale light in one section. Bulky, brass lanterns that needed to be lit with matches in another. One section required Gram to spin a crank for a few seconds until dim amber lights came to life.

Further in, the lighting stopped, but the strong glow from massive numbers of phosphorescent rocks created an unreal beauty to guide their way. Shortly after, they reached a section of pure dark. Sully handed out flashlights. With slow, cautious steps they made their way through until they reached an area that resembled a playground — filled with nooks and tunnels and overpasses.

Sunlight bounced around. Elliot glanced back at Roni. "There are a lot of sections with natural light like this. As far as we know, nobody in the Society has ever located the source. Perhaps you'll discover it someday."

But no matter how beautiful the sights, no matter how amazing the history, eventually, the excitement lessened. They trudged along through more and more dark sections with little to see. They stayed quiet, focusing on the next step, and the next, and the next. The click of their walking, the jangle of their equipment, the clump of the donkey-golem echoed into the distance making a unique, cavern music. But even that sprinkling sound could not relieve the drudgery of doing nothing but walking.

By the time Gram called the day to an end, Roni's mind had become a dull blankness nearly as dark as the lightless cavern sections. Scanning the area, she saw that Gram had picked a concave section of a large rock wall for their rest.

A knee-high edge of stones had been formed by previous explorers. It took a crescent shape, and Sully went to work building a fire in the center — he had brought wood for this purpose but also warned that as they went further, they would be wise to pick up anything usable for the future.

Once he had a steady fire going, he removed a cooking pot, several bags of vegetables and meat, a box of spices, and a jug of water. "I hope you all are up for some stew. If not, you can eat it anyway because I'm not taking requests."

Elliot and Gram examined the map printouts Roni had brought. They murmured to each other as they pointed out various sections.

And Roni — she rubbed her sore shoulders as she rested on a large, flat rock. Flexing her toes, she knew to keep her boots on and laced. If she took them off, chances were her feet would swell to the point that it would be difficult, if not impossible, to put her boots back on.

After about twenty minutes, she rose and dug out her new journal from her backpack. She hovered a pen over the first fresh, blank page. She wrote:

*I don't know what to write.*

Bemused, she took a breath and gazed at the Old Gang. They all acted so calm and in control. She wondered how many times they had ventured into these caverns. Maybe one day, she too would act the same.

Resetting her pen to paper, she wrote:

*My head is too full to know the best way to begin. Having spent a year reading the journals of other Society members before me, I feel that I should offer something profound in these pages. Maybe someday I will. Others have written journals that are poetic, vivid, and just far better than anything I could write. Still, this is my duty, I suppose, and I want to do it. I want to let the future Society members know what our lives were like, and as my experience grows, to know what I learn so that readers can learn, too. But as far as my first day hiking goes, I can only say that I am happy to finally be on my way. My feet ache and my muscles are cramped. I stink. Yet I can't wait to get back at it tomorrow. To whoever will read this, I hope my first entry is enough.*

She read over her words, grabbed the page, and nearly ripped it out. But before she could do so, she heard a strange sound. Something nearby hissed. Roni bolted upright and caught Gram staring at a spot off to the left. Snapping her fingers, Gram pulled Elliot and Sully's attention.

A bone-white creature skittered onto a rock. It had the wrinkled, scrawny look of a furless cat and an overall alabaster coloring. On some parts — especially around the mouth — the skin bordered on translucent. Though no bigger than a terrier, the creature's movements reminded Roni of a gorilla. Black, raisin eyes darted from Roni to Gram to the boys. Once again, it hissed, revealing a mouthful of teeth like jagged rocks.

"It's okay," Roni said as if talking to a frightened dog. She smiled at the creature and moved closer. "We won't hurt you."

"Roni, freeze," Gram said. The creature backed away at the harsh voice.

Sully said, "Perhaps I can —"

"No. You stay by Roni. Keep her safe."

Roni looked over at Gram. "Safe? It's just a little —"

The creature jumped onto a rock closer to Roni. She stumbled back, unable to stop the surprised screech from escaping her lips. Just a short sound, but enough to scare the creature. Sully put his hands on Roni's shoulders, steadying her with his firm stance.

The creature thrust out its chest and hissed. Gram moved towards it, her arms out as if she intended to tackle the thing should it leap forward. Locking her eyes on the creature's every movement, Gram said, "Elliot, get me the green book from the donkey-golem."

Elliot nodded and cautiously backed away. Gram stepped forward. The creature rocked its shoulders before moving in a tight circle. It clearly did not like the situation, but it also did not appear willing to back down.

"Elliot?" Gram said. Her right arm lowered and her hand pulled into her sleeve.

"Got it," he said, coming up to her side. He held a large green book similar to all the books chained to the walls.

Roni saw Gram's wrist twitch and she put it all together. "Don't do that," she said.

But Gram's arm had already begun its motion. She snapped out her hand and a chain flew from her sleeve. It caught the creature's ankle and tightened around the bone. As the creature shrieked, Gram transferred her end of the chain to her free hand. Then she shot out another chain. This one caught the creature around the chest.

Crying like a lost child, the creature leaned back, pulling uselessly on the chains. Though Gram could not hold her ground like Sully, she had no trouble keeping this small creature under control.

Gram cocked her head back. "Open the book!"

Elliot held the book facing the creature and pulled back the cover. Roni reached up for Sully's hand and braced herself. She had seen books opened before — they could vacuum in everything around them.

But nothing happened. No whoosh of air. No howling winds. No vortex pulling one universe into another.

Elliot planted one foot against a rock behind him. "Now!"

Yelling like a warrior, Gram swung the creature straight into the open book. She released the chains, allowing the entire package to pass into the pages. The sound of the creature screaming weakened as if it fell down a long shaft. Elliot shut the cover and Gram hurried over to tie a fresh chain around the outside.

Roni wrenched free from Sully. "What the hell did you do?"

"Watch your language," Gram said.

"That thing was just scared and you tossed it away like it meant nothing."

"That thing is a relic — a living relic. You remember what that is?"

With an impatient sigh, Roni said, "Yes. A relic is an object from another universe that gets stuck in ours."

Gram took the book over to the donkey-golem and roughly made room to store it. "Well, relics can be living things, too. Yal-hara is a relic, and so was that thing. It doesn't belong here."

Stomping over, Roni said, "And does it belong in that book? Is that where it came from?"

"Of course not. This book opens to an empty universe. I use it for all the things that I cannot place anywhere else."

"Shouldn't we at least have tried to find where this thing came from? You just tossed it away. Threw it into — what? What's *an empty universe?* Unless that's a euphemism for a thriving ecosystem, I'm guessing that creature is going to die floating in emptiness." She looked to Elliot and Sully. "Are you guys really okay with this? Is that how you've all been handling things? Just sweeping the relics under the rug?"

Sully stabbed a finger in her direction. "Young lady, you should learn to close your mouth and open your ears. You don't know what you're talking about right now."

"I know that murdering a creature because it's in our universe isn't right."

Gram's stern brow eased as she approached. She hooked her arm through Roni's. "Let's take a little walk. The boys will clean up."

Though anger urged Roni to rip her arm away and yell more, the sensible side of her prevailed. She had not seen Gram like this since before she joined the Society. A dim light deep inside her warmed at her grandmother's kind touch. It had been too long. Patting Gram's hand, she nodded, and together they went for a walk.

At first, they stayed silent. Their footsteps echoed around them. Just as when Roni was little, Gram had the ability to time things right. Before the silence grew uncomfortable, Gram spoke in a calm, soothing voice.

"I know this part is going to be hard for you. It was for me, too."

"You can't possibly convince me that —"

"Shhh. Let me speak. The first thing you must understand is that in order to protect our universe, we must get rid of all relics as fast as possible. Remember that each relic brings with it the threat of germs, bacteria, even seeds of invasive species — all of which could wipe us out, if we are not careful."

"What about Yal-hara?"

"Some relics, like her, predate my involvement with the Society. Any damage those relics would do has already been done."

Remembering that Gram had a private stash of relic

alcohol, Roni snickered. "Is that why you don't mind having vodka from another universe in the bookstore?"

"You can laugh at me, but yes, that's true. Now, pay attention. These caverns are not part of our universe."

"I know. I read about it in Waterfield's journal."

"What you may not know is that there are no living things in this universe. I do not know how the caverns came into existence. I believe our Lord provided them, but that doesn't mean He made them. However it happened, the caverns are here to house the books. Nothing more. When we come across a relic, especially a living relic, we must dispose of it as fast as possible — because if a relic can devastate our universe, mankind dies; but if it devastates these caverns —"

"Then everything dies." Roni paused as she looked at all the books hanging from the walls. "All of it. Holy shit."

Gram smacked Roni's hand. "Please. I'm not stupid enough to think you don't cuss all the time, but I don't need to hear it."

"Sorry." A thought hit her, and Roni faced Gram. "If the caverns are a different universe, doesn't that make us relics in here, too?"

"You understand now. We are just as dangerous to everything in here. It is why we must be extremely careful — not only to protect the caverns, but to protect ourselves. We don't know how large the caverns are, but it has been suggested that they connect all universes. If that is true, it stands to reason that there are other Parallel Society-type organizations out there, and if we come across one, then they may try to dispose of us, fearing the damage we may cause in here."

"So you got rid of that creature both to save the caverns but also because it might try to throw us in a book?"

"Exactly."

All the sounds bouncing off the walls, the glorious symphony of clicks and drips and unidentified tinkling tones, no longer brought joy. Roni shifted on her feet. Could there be another Society out there? Watching her? Waiting to chain her up and toss her away?

"Let's go back," she said. They turned around and walked toward the campfire. "If we're potentially damaging the caverns by being here, then why are we doing it? I don't mean this time, I get that we're helping Yal-hara, and I guess Elliot, too — and you've got to explain that one to me soon — but what about all those expeditions of the past?"

"For hundreds of years, I doubt anybody understood what damage they might cause. It's only been in the twentieth century that the concept of the multiverse has come to be. I've tried to limit our exposure in here as much as possible. I can only pray that you will have the sense and ability to put rules into place that will further protect these caverns."

"Me?"

"As you've pointed out numerous times, we're getting old. You know you're taking over for us eventually. This is one thing you need to start thinking about."

When they returned, Elliot and Sully had cleaned up all evidence of their meal. Sleeping bags had been unrolled, and both men had curled up for the night. Gram indicated one of the bags for Roni.

After everyone wished pleasant dreams, the Old Gang fell asleep fast. But Roni could not. Her mind swirled with all that had happened and all that Gram had said.

On the one hand, she felt thrilled to have come so far, to have seen deeper into the caverns, to have witnessed a living relic, and experienced her first day of adventure. On the other hand, Gram had finally given in a little and offered Roni a touch of responsibility. And what was it? Find rules that more or less shut down her access to the very thing that makes everything exciting and worthwhile. On the other, other hand, she accepted the seriousness of her task and would do her best. On the other, other, other hand, the whole thing ticked her off. Because once again, Gram had taken charge, and in doing so, changed the way the entire trip had gone.

Roni punched her pillow a few times and thrust her head down. Sleep would not be coming soon, and every sound threatened to attack her as if she were the dangerous relic. A small voice in the back of her head wondered if they shouldn't simply turn around and go home.

# CHAPTER 10

When Roni woke, Elliot and Sully had already begun to pack up for the day. Waking in a cavern disoriented her — no sunlight, no change in temperature, nothing but another hour. Gram nibbled on a pumpernickel roll nearby.

Roni stood and felt an unwelcome pressure below. She crawled over to Gram. Whispering, she said, "Um, I have to go to the bathroom."

"So? Go. You didn't have a problem yesterday."

"That was all number one. I have to really go, this time."

Gram winked. "It doesn't make a difference. Go behind a rock and let loose."

"But what about everything you said? Isn't it dangerous to leave our business here? Germs and bacteria and everything?"

"Dear, if poo is going to destroy this universe, it would already have happened. You think the Society members of a hundred years ago thought about such things?"

"I guess not. It doesn't seem right, though. Shouldn't we be better?"

"We try to be. When it comes to this, unless you brought a doggie poop bag, you've got two choices. Either go behind the rocks and do your business, or take one of my empty books and squat into that."

Roni opted to go behind the rocks. She thought she'd be a hypocrite if she crapped into another universe — even an empty universe — to be clean in this one. As she headed off, Sully called her name. She looked up and he tossed over a roll of toilet paper.

Shortly afterward, the group finished packing and they started on the day's hike. This time, the allure of the caverns had faded. Roni still found interesting rock formations and unusual ways light bounced around, but the excitement and majesty of her first steps drifted further behind.

Each minute brought pain — her feet had blistered and her muscles ached. She grew thirsty but avoided taking more than the minimum of water. Partly because she wanted to ration what they had, and partly because she decided that morning to avoid going to the bathroom as much as possible.

Elliot put up a hand to stop the hike. Using his cane, he drew a line across the dirt at his feet. "Our maps end here. We may have to go slower from time to time because it has been many years since I have traveled this way. It will all come back to me, so please have patience."

"Of course," Sully said. "We understand."

Roni wanted to yell that she didn't understand, that nobody would tell her what was Elliot's problem with this Isle, but she stayed quiet. As they powered onward, she pulled out her journal and attempted to keep a rough detail of the path. She figured that even if her entries never became worthwhile reading material, at least she could provide useful maps.

"Good idea," Sully said, walking side-by-side with his donkey-golem. "If the world this Book on the Isle leads to is half as wonderful to view as I have heard, we will certainly want to know how to get back."

Roni thought about what she had read in Waterfield's journal. When he discovered the book, he wrote down what he saw when he looked inside.

> *A marvel to behold. Bright with gold and silver. People much like ourselves, only filled with light and joy. They dressed in flowing gowns that declared their freedom as much as the happiness upon their faces. From my vantage point, I witnessed a gorgeous fountain in the center of a town that seemed to be in an agrarian utopia. A true fantasy lifted from one of our children's books, only nary a witch or evil giant in sight.*

For the next hour, their path led them along the base of a cliff. Roni kept expecting rocks to fall from above, but nothing so dangerous occurred. Even the books above her were chained tight against the walls.

Later, the ground sloped downward — a smooth descent that slowed their progress. The path spiraled downward as if they navigated their way through the inside of a long tube. Books swung from chains above them. Some hung so low, Roni and the others had to duck in order to pass.

Until they reached the halfway point.

Gram gasped and they halted. "What happened?"

The pathway forward had all the chains jingling against each other, but no books. Some chains had been torn free from the ceiling. Some of the links dotted the ground. But every last book had been removed — only the chains remained.

Elliot slid his cane across several of the hanging chains,

creating an eerie music. "I have never seen such a thing. Sully?"

Pushing his way forward, Sully inspected the chains. "I haven't. But this doesn't look natural."

"Of course it's not natural," Gram said.

"I only meant that the books didn't fall, the chains didn't rust or weaken. And if I had to say, I would wager that these books were violently ripped loose."

Gram nodded. "So it wasn't somebody like us — somebody with the kinds of powers we have."

Sully's focus drifted toward Roni. "We must be extra careful."

Roni wished she could muster a light comment, some way to dismiss the fear circulating amongst them, but she only managed to swallow hard against her dry throat.

They proceeded further down. All the chains without books swayed like nooses without bodies — a threat hanging with each one. At the bottom, the ground leveled into an open plain of rocks. Thankfully, the books there remained. A few were missing from the lower sections of the walls, but the majority of the spaces had books properly chained — as far as they could tell. The ceiling of this cavern section rose so high, it became lost to the dark.

Unfortunately, the ground could be seen with total clarity. Relics like the living one that had stumbled upon their campsite the night before littered the ground. Only these no longer lived. Hundreds of pale corpses had been spread across the dirt, each one twisted in an agonized position. Their foul odor rose in the air.

Gram covered her mouth. Elliot looked away. Sully glanced downward and shook his head.

"What did this?" Roni asked.

Patting her cross against her chest, Gram said, "We will find out. Elliot, please locate the source of this evil."

Stepping forward, Elliot lifted his cane horizontal over one of the corpses. He wrinkled his nose at the sharp stench. Closing his eyes, he raised his hand and also held it horizontal to the corpse. After a few quiet moments, he lowered his hands and stepped forward, placing each foot with care. When he stopped walking, he lifted his cane and hand as before. This continued for several minutes. Each time, he moved deeper and deeper into the slaughter.

While they waited, Roni tried to jot down notes in her journal, but finding the words to describe this horror failed her. She kept seeing the living relic Gram had tossed into a book and wondered if that creature had been escaping whatever had caused this. Everywhere she looked, she saw accusing glares as if the dead might rise and point at her and blame her for the death of their friend.

*Don't be stupid,* she thought. She had done nothing wrong. If anybody, Gram deserved such glares, yet that wasn't even true — Gram did not mass murder these creatures.

By the time Elliot returned, Roni needed any distraction from the surrounding death. "So?" she said, the eagerness in her voice mimicked by the hopeful looks from Gram and Sully.

Elliot's grim countenance answered before he spoke. "I cannot get a clear reading. All the books around us, all the books in these massive caverns, they lead to near-infinite universes. It is too much to narrow my focus. When I know which book we are searching for, I can handle it. One universe is difficult, but possible. Here there is simply too much pulling me in all directions. Especially because there is a good, logical possibility that these once-living relics came from one of the books now missing."

"Thank you for trying," Gram said. "Let's move on. We've still got plenty of hiking to do, and Lord knows I don't want to smell these things any longer. Everybody be vigilant."

With that, they left. Roni wanted to ask why they didn't dispose of the bodies. Shouldn't they be worried about contaminating the caverns? But evidence pointed out that despite Gram's warnings, the caverns had been exposed to much over the centuries, and while it behooved them all to be better custodians, Roni would not have to worry over every germ.

They trudged onward for several hours until Gram finally pointed to a trickle of water running off of a large boulder. "We'll camp here."

Once they had eaten and settled in, the Old Gang again fell asleep with ease. Roni, however, could not shake the heaviness in her thoughts. The dead relics troubled her, but more, her mind rattled through scenarios of her future — none of which ended with good results.

She was expected to learn how to do things yet Gram withheld too much information. Then, when she finally did learn a few things, Gram contradicted her rules with blatant disregard in her actions. Roni had always been a believer in the idea that one had to know the rules before breaking them. It helped to avoid stupid mistakes. Yet it seemed that one day she would be inheriting all the responsibilities of the Parallel Society with no firm grasp on the basics. And no matter how many times she played that idea, she couldn't help but wonder if part of Gram wanted her to fail. Maybe it helped Gram still feel useful.

Roni rolled onto her side, but she could not clear her mind. Yet at some point in the night, her thoughts became her dreams, and the hours slipped by. The next thing Roni knew, Elliot nudged her awake.

He smiled at her scrunched face. "Hurry up. We are close. Today, if I can still find the entrance, we will arrive at the Book on the Isle."

Twenty minutes later, they had the campsite clean and the donkey-golem packed. Elliot moved with an exuberant step as he led the way further into the caverns. Despite his excitement, Roni kept her own expectations low. Good thing, too. It would be three hours before they reached a dark passageway with a hole in the side.

"Here, here," Elliot said, waving a flashlight. "Be careful. This is rugged."

The ground angled downward on a series of large rocks poking out at odd angles. Roni did her best to help Gram and Elliot work their way to the bottom. Sully's ability to hold to the ground like a redwood rooted for five hundred years kept him stable. He guided the donkey-golem.

Before they reached the bottom, Roni heard the gentle sound of water streaming over stones. She smelled the freshness in the air and felt the moisture surrounding her. "This is really it," she said.

"Yes," Elliot said, beaming his flashlight across the water. "It has been a very long time, yet this looks the same as when I last saw it. How wondrous."

Roni walked to the edge and knelt. "Is it safe to drink?"

"Absolutely."

She smiled and dunked her head in the cool current of Waterfield River. It felt like all the ugliness they had seen washed away. She drank a little — tastelessly fresh. When she resurfaced, her whirling thoughts settled. Not far away, they would find the book. She would reach in and pluck out a kyolo stone. Her first big mission, and she would not only succeed in helping Yal-hara, but she might be able to help herself recover some memories. She wanted to cheer, but Gram would not appreciate that, so Roni dunked her head once more.

"Enough already," Gram said when Roni came back up

for air. "This is not the time to start bathing. We've got a lot of work to do before we get on the water."

"We do?"

"Sure. We can't possibly take the donkey-golem with us, and that means we can't take all our supplies. Time to make some hard choices."

# CHAPTER 11

As Gram pulled items from the donkey-golem's saddle bags, Sully brought out two inflatable rafts and two air pumps. Elliot joined Gram separating needed items from those that would stay behind. So, Roni inferred where they expected her to work. Grabbing a raft, she got busy unrolling it, attaching the air pump nozzle, and then pumping over and over to inflate the raft.

"Everybody gets to keep one change of clothes," Gram announced.

Roni kept pumping. "Just pick something from my bag. It doesn't matter."

At length, she and Sully finished the rafts and set them in the water. All four helped load their limited supplies on the two rafts. Then Gram pointed at Sully. "You and I will take the back. Elliot and Roni, take the lead."

As Roni climbed into the front boat and Gram took the back, Sully and Elliot picked up the supplies staying behind and put them on the donkey-golem. Sully leaned over and whispered to the creature. Snorting, the donkey-golem turned around and clambered up into the dark.

When Sully climbed in his raft, he said, "Our things will

be waiting for us back at the bookstore."

"Is everyone ready?" Elliot said, taking the front position. "Then let us begin."

Pushing off the shore, Roni had the urge to point out that they had begun days ago, but instead, she used an orange, plastic paddle to help guide them along the river. Unlike hiking through the caverns, traveling upon the water filled the air with constant sounds. The simplest babble of water over stone echoed and amplified. Paddle strokes and subtle splashes became long-lasting noise. Even the groups' breathing played back upon them.

"Be careful ahead. Duck," Elliot said.

Roni scooted lower in the back of the raft, and a moment later, they passed under a rock bridge that reached close to the water at parts. If she hadn't listened, she would have cracked her head against the stone. The current picked up as they curved off to the right. The next section opened wider, and to Roni's surprise, there were numerous chained books to be found.

"How did these get here? I mean, do you guys regularly use rafts to find places to chain these books?"

From behind, Gram said, "Not our doing. Possibly not even our Society. Don't forget that the odds favor there being other Societies from other universes." She gestured with her oar. "You can see some pathways going off, so this river isn't the only way to get in here."

Something in the air above squeaked. Roni popped on her flashlight and caught a glimpse of a bat-like creature flapping its way from one stalactite to another. Once it came to rest, it stretched out its wings — all four of them.

"I guess you can't really catch those relics," Roni said.

Sully chuckled. "You'd be surprised what we can accomplish."

"Should we stop, then, and take care of those things?"

"Oh, so now you want to throw relics into books?"

"I only want to do our job. And I doubt those creatures want to end up like the dead ones we saw yesterday."

"No," Elliot said. "We must keep going. Relics like those have their own fates to follow."

Gram said, "C'mon, Roni. You're the one keeping the journal. Make a note, and we'll come back someday to take care of it. There's only so many problems we can handle at once."

Roni agreed — partially because she understood how difficult it would be to catch flying creatures so far above them, partially because she knew Elliot needed to keep on track, and partially because by the time they had finished chatting about it, the river had already pushed them towards a new section of the caverns. Roni noticed the current had strengthened, and Elliot concentrated on steering. They bumped hard against something — a rock, most likely — and Elliot shoved them off to the right. The noise level increased, too. The constant echo doubled, then tripled, then quadrupled the river's growing rage.

"Left! Left!" Elliot bellowed over his shoulder.

Roni tried to paddle the way he wanted, but the raft heaved upward and splashed down like hitting cold steel. The jolt sent electric sparks up her spine. Her fingers clenched involuntarily, and for two seconds, she could not get her body to follow her commands.

"Your other left!" Elliot said, not having time to look back.

They smacked into an outcrop of stones. The hit spun them until they were facing Gram and Sully while zipping backwards down the river. Sully's flashlight jittered across their faces, and Roni saw how ghost pale they both looked. Water flooded over the edges of the raft, soaking her as she fought the current to turn them around — she needed to get them going in the right direction, and she didn't want to see Gram's fear any longer than necessary.

The bottom dropped out from under her. One moment, she dug her paddle into the water, and the next, the water disappeared and they fell. Only a few feet, but her stomach rose straight up her throat. This time, she had the luck to raise her body before slamming into the water. Though this saved her from another spine-wrenching jolt, the action also left her unbalanced. Her body fell sideways, folding over the edge of the raft. As she raised her head to get back, she saw the cavern wall — right before it smacked her in the forehead.

Bright lights flashed before her eyes as the pain radiated across her face, down her back, and through her legs. The metallic taste of blood wet her mouth, and the side of her tongue throbbed. Something grabbed hold of her and yanked her back into the raft. She gazed upward. The dark image of Elliot with the darkness of the cavern behind him tilted as he looked upon her.

"Are you okay?" he asked.

She had no idea how many times he asked the question, but her head finally cleared enough for her to nod. "I will be," she said, reaching for her plastic oar. "Get back up front. We need to watch where —"

The front of the raft flew upward as if it skied along a ramp. Elliot tumbled onto Roni as a loud pop burst out followed by the hissing of air leaking from their raft.

"Quickly," Elliot said as he scrambled toward the front. He wrapped the head of the raft in his arms, hugging it tightly as he attempted to slow the loss of air. "Grab what you can. Toss it to Sully."

Roni threw her backpack onto her shoulders and picked up a box of food. She looked back, but didn't see Gram and Sully. The floor of the raft dipped deeper into the river and the fast-moving waters pooled in.

"It is of no use," Elliot said, letting the front go. He gathered two boxes, one on each shoulder, stuck his cane under one arm, and hopped into the water. It went up to his chest, but he managed to hold his ground.

Roni had no choice but to follow. Her head only came up to his chest under normal conditions, so she held her breath as she jumped in. The box broke free from her grasp as if a giant tore it away. Water rushed up her nose. Sputtering, she thrust her hands outward and attempt to spin around so that she floated on her back with her feet leading the way.

Too dark to see anybody, too noisy to hear anything clearly, she rode the river until the current eased off. When the waters no longer threatened to pulverize her against the rocks, she rolled over and swam to the shore. Coughing, she crawled out. Then the cool air sent shivers across her skin.

"Elliot?" she gasped. "Gram?" From her water-logged backpack, she pulled out a penlight and flashed it upriver. "Sully?"

"Over here," a voice called out — Gram!

The Old Gang paddled to the shore with Elliot hanging on the side. They all climbed out and flopped onto the gravel edge.

"Well," Sully said, "that definitely didn't go well. Remind me, no whitewater rafting with you lot."

Gram chuckled. "We still have the one raft. That's good."

"And we lost half of our supplies — including my change of clothes, I might add."

"Complain all you want once we get back on the water. Come on. Help me with Roni. She's been through a lot."

Roni waved them off. "I'm fine. Soaked, but fine. Just

give me a few minutes."

"We can't stay here."

Gram's odd tone sent a different shiver across Roni's skin. Sully reached toward Elliot to help him reorganize the raft. As they made room for all four, Roni used her penlight to scan the cavern. She didn't smell or hear anything irregular, but her skin continued prickling long after it should have eased back.

"Is something out there?" she whispered.

A pale red light formed on the cavern walls. Roni snapped off her penlight as the red grew brighter. The walls themselves appeared to thin — as if they were flesh with lights behind the skin. Chained books swung from these skin walls and a deep rumbling rose on the air. Roni and Gram hustled to help with the raft, and in less than a minute they were ready.

As they pushed off, Roni caught sight of several chains without books. Gram noticed it, too. She then pointed near where they had stopped. Holes big enough to fit a kid's plastic pool dotted the ground. In the distance, Roni saw a shadowy form stretching up towards the ceiling. She swore it moved, and she wondered if those holes in the ground had been made by the shadow's feet. What kind of creature could make such a mark?

Shaking off the winding path her mind had taken her, she looked again. Yes, there was a shadow, but it did not move. Perhaps no more than a flicker of light, but it was no creature. It couldn't have been.

Sully paddled in the back while Elliot steered up front. Moments later, the river curved off and the horrid sight disappeared behind them.

Roni stared at the dying red embers in the distance. "Will one of you explain that to me?"

Digging a blanket out of their meager supplies and

handing it to Roni, Gram said, "That was another universe. From the looks of it, not a place I'd like to visit."

"Are you serious?"

Keeping his focus forward, Elliot said, "Do you really think this is a time we would choose to joke with you?"

"I meant that ... well, I don't know. How could that have been a separate universe?"

"We do not know how any of this cavern works exactly, but from what I have read and seen, I believe this river acts as a conduit between caverns. In other words, the caverns that hold the books are not all one endless structure but rather, it is a connection of structures spread over many universes. The river is one method of traveling between them."

"You're saying we're not in our own universe anymore?"

Sully said, "Our cavern isn't even in our universe. I thought you knew that already."

"I did. I do. I just — this is a bit much to take in." Her body wobbled, and Gram held her to make sure she didn't flop backward into the river. "So, we saw part of a universe in that section of cave, and we're now in another universe? And this whole cavern system is several universes?"

Sully grinned. "See that? You're smart, after all."

Gram said, "It's another reason we don't worry about contaminating the caverns too much. They are a mixture of universes by their very nature. Though it's still good practice to keep our end of things as clean as possible."

Holding the blanket on her shoulders a bit closer, Roni said, "How do you know all this? From what I saw in the Grand Library, none of you have spent much time down there."

"We did when we were younger, back when we had a librarian. And as far as we know, well, it's what's written in the books. I've often thought that much of it all is educated guesswork."

Elliot added, "There have been some attempts at using the scientific method to test out our ideas. While nothing conclusive has been determined, this is the best explanation we have so far."

"Best thing is to remember that the caverns are dangerous on more levels than we even know. Don't explore it lightly."

Roni looked up at Elliot. He knew how difficult this journey could become, yet he not only offered to help Roni, but he encouraged her. She opened her mouth to ask him directly or to point out this fact, but then her mouth closed. Elliot had turned back with a broad smile.

"We have arrived," he said.

# CHAPTER 12

Rock walls spread out in all directions to form an enormous cave too far across to see the end. The river let into a lake that filled most of the cavern space. Large enough to create real waves, the lake must have been several miles wide. Oddly, the air felt warmer and smelled salty.

Elliot whooped — a strange sound to hear coming from him. "We made it. I do not think I ever truly believed I would see this place again. But we made it."

As the water pushed them closer to one wall, Roni noticed ledges with stairs running alongside. A few of these stony paths led to openings, but she could only see darkness inside the passageways — if that was what they were. The echoes of the cave had changed from the rest of the caverns. Perhaps because of its size, their voices echoed less, the sounds dying off quicker. Perhaps not — Roni did not know auditory physics. She only knew for certain that the quality of sound had altered.

Something else bothered her. She could not pinpoint her discomfort until Sully said, "Where are all the books?"

Not a single book had been placed on the walls. These books, however, had not been ripped down by unseen hands. They simply never existed in the first place. No chains hung from above, no marks in the walls, no shelves — nothing to indicate that a book to another universe had ever been there.

Roni thought about something she had read in Waterfield's journal. Some books, some universes, were more powerful than others. Some required more chains. Some had to be buried in stone. But the Book on the Isle had to be alone.

"This whole cave," Roni said, "and the lake and all of it — this is to contain only the one book. It's a prison."

"No, dear," Gram said. "It is an oasis."

"Over there," Elliot said, pointing toward the center of the lake. "Everybody, please help."

Sully dug out two extra paddles and handed them over. Roni leaned across the right side of the inflated raft while Gram took the left. With all four digging into the water, they moved exactly where Elliot indicated. Despite the extra muscle and the increase in speed, they still traveled for a half-hour before Roni saw it — the Isle.

More like a glorified sand dune — at least, it appeared so in the dim light produced from their flashlights and two shafts of daylight ricocheting in from parts unknown. The closer they came, the less she saw on the isle. From afar, she thought she saw brush, maybe a tree, but with every paddle stroke, Roni realized the isle truly lacked all but sand.

And a pedestal.

When they hit the shore, Elliot swung his legs over the front of the raft. Roni got out to help him bring the raft up into the sand. As Sully and Gram worked their way over the sides, Roni followed Elliot inland for several feet.

There, toppled like a fallen tree, the remnants of a stone pedestal lay. The sand surrounding the stones had been disturbed, too. But they weren't footprints — not human ones anyway. In fact, the more Roni inspected the area, the more her stomach churned. The prints were holes in the ground. Not as large as a kid's plastic pool, but similar in shape and depth.

"It is here," Elliot said as Gram approached. He stood a foot from the top end of the pedestal. Pointing to a chained book, he said, "This is it."

Roni gestured to the marks in the sand. "Something found your oasis."

Gram patted her cross as she stared at the prints. She then gave a short nod. Roni fought hard to keep her face still. She tamped down any excitement rising from the mere idea that Gram would acknowledge something she said as valuable — especially because that excitement bothered her. She didn't want to care what Gram thought. She couldn't. Not when she had to be on her own.

Sully arrived and set right the pedestal's stone base. In order to keep her cool, Roni launched into helping. Gram picked up the book and looked it over. As Roni handed stones to Sully, she heard Gram and Elliot talking.

"I don't think you should do this," Gram said.

"You know I must. Why come all the way out here if we are not going to open the book?"

"That was before we saw the conditions of this place."

"So what if the book was knocked over? Anything could have flown in here and done it by accident."

"You don't believe that. And even if you somehow convince yourself of it, Lord knows I don't believe it. I'm not sure I can condone the risks you're going to take."

Elliot pecked at the sand with his cane. "I find it amusing that you speak as if you have a say in the matter."

"I'm still the leader of this team." Gram stepped in front of Elliot and spoke in a harsh whisper that Roni and Sully could hear even easier than the previous conversation. "We are here because of Roni, not you. All of your issues with this place are a side matter that I am happy to see you address, but that is not the mission."

"Not for you."

"Elliot, please don't do this. Don't start making poor decisions because you feel guilty."

"It was my poor decision that cost me —"

"I know that. But you are not alone here. This isn't all on your shoulders, and it isn't about you. Sully is here. I'm here. You care about us, right? And most importantly, Roni is here. I know you care about her. Are you willing to put her at risk just so you can feel better about something so far in the past that you're not even that man anymore?"

Elliot puffed his chest and gazed over Gram's head. "I do not expect you to understand, but I must do this. Roni has her own mission, one that I can help her with, but even if she decides against, I will still go."

Brushing sand from her hands as she stood, Roni presumed a dark cloud would form over her head when she said, "Go where?"

Gram turned around with such shock on her face that Roni stepped back. Elliot also looked at her like she had mushrooms growing out of her nose. With the top of his cane, he bumped the book in Gram's arms and said, "In there, of course. We go into the book."

# CHAPTER 13

If Roni had eaten anything substantial in the last day, she would have thrown it up twice over. She paced the sandy isle while Elliot sat near the pedestal. With his eyes closed, he meditated. During the entire trip, she had assumed she would reach into the book with one hand, grab the kyolo stones, and that would be it. Never did she think they would physically enter the books. Why didn't anybody tell her? She wanted to shake Elliot, yell at him, get him to smile or get some words of confidence from him, hit him, hug him, anything to shock the energy out of her system. She paced faster.

During these minutes, Gram and Sully conferred near the raft. Roni's attention volleyed between them and Elliot and the book. It had a tattered cover of red and black circles. Two holes remained from where the original chains had kept it bound to the pedestal.

Roni could picture the thing opening. The horrors she had seen when gazing through a book flashed in her mind. Yes, she knew that Waterfield's journal described it as a paradise. And yes, Elliot would not be jumping into a book that led to a nightmare. But those points of reason did little to assuage her growing unease.

"We're ready," Sully said as he walked towards the pedestal.

Elliot snapped awake and jumped to his feet. He gave a slight bow toward Sully, then Gram, then Roni. "I thank you all for helping me in this endeavor." Before Gram could speak, he raised his hand. "I know you believe that you are doing this not for me but for the Society. Perhaps that is true. Perhaps you are, and I am being naive. But I thank you anyway."

Gram flicked her wrist and a chain fell from her sleeve. And it continued to fall. The non-stop ringing of metal on metal as it piled at her feet sounded like coins dropping from a slot machine. When it finally finished, she handed the end to Sully. He wrapped it around himself and used the teeth-like clamp on the end to secure it. Elliot pulled out the other end of the chain and offered it to Roni.

The cold metal weighed more than she anticipated. Gram must be worried about the strain. Roni refrained from making any comment — she didn't need the Old Gang knowing her fearful thoughts, and any word from her might betray the shaking in her legs. As she locked the chain around her waist, she could hear it jangling in her hands. To hide the sound, she asked Elliot, "What about you?"

Gram released another chain. This one, though equally thick, was much shorter. She handed one end to Elliot, and as he secured it, she clamped the other end to Roni's chain. "You two will have to take care of each other."

Sully shoved one foot into the sand, then the other. He closed his eyes, mouthed a few words, then leaned back slightly. Roni knew he could summon the strength of a golem to root himself to the ground, but she had no clue how long it would last.

As Gram settled the book upon the pedestal, Elliot nudged Roni's arm with his cane. "Time for us to go."

They walked towards the pedestal, and Roni's throat tightened. She wiped her palms against her sides. Brushing the chain, she felt its weight tugging behind.

"Listen close," Gram said. Her voice took on the same tone she used years ago when laying down the rules for a sleepover. Only with this, if Roni broke a rule, serious consequences would follow — not a grounding or a loss of television privileges, but injury or death. "You are to tug on the chain three times every five minutes to let us know you're okay. If you fail to do so, we will yank you right back here and that'll be it. No going back in."

"Hold on," Roni said. "Do you mean tug on it three times in a row at the end of five minutes or three times throughout a five minute period?"

"I mean three times in five minutes. What's so hard to understand?"

"I don't want you pulling us back if we're not ready."

Sully forced out a laugh. "Okay, you two, keep this simple. Three times in a row roughly every five minutes. Clear enough?"

"Thank you," Roni said.

Gram shot a harsh glare at Sully before continuing. "If you run into trouble, just keeping tugging over and over as fast as possible. Is that clear enough? It will be to us. Roni, you get in there, grab your kyolo stones, and wait for Elliot. The less you interact, the safer for you and for that universe. Elliot, do what you must but don't you dare put Roni at risk."

"I would never put her at risk."

"You already have by bringing her here."

"I am only going to talk with them. Nothing more. There is no risk to be had."

"Nonetheless, you know what to do if you have to."

Elliot nodded. "Of course."

"Good luck," Gram said and rested her hands on the book. She gripped it tight. Roni got the distinct impression that Gram considered throwing the book into the lake. But her shoulders dropped with a sigh. "Good luck," she whispered and opened the book.

Roni flinched, but all remained still. Nothing but quiet. A thick mist rolled over the edges of the book, and with it a strong smell of thyme.

Reading the confusion on her face, Elliot said, "Not all universes depressurize when a book is opened. Some are close enough to our world — or in this case, to the world of this cave. It is no more than opening a door."

"So, we can walk in and out without any trouble?"

"Exactly."

Putting words in action, Elliot stepped toward the book. Roni did not wait for the chain to pull her along. She hurried up to Elliot's side and clasped his hand. His excitement vibrated in his fingers, and the corners of her mouth lifted. Several stones had been piled into a small step. Together, they climbed up.

Though the book looked about the width of a library dictionary, Roni could not see how they would fit in. But when Elliot placed his left leg inside, the rest of him smeared as if his image flickered on ruined film. He didn't scream or show any sign of pain. The colors of him ran together and poured into the book.

Roni followed — had no choice with the chain connecting them — and to her shock, she felt nothing. Despite the bizarre picture she had seen, experiencing the effect caused no sensation at all. She simply walked into the book.

She did her best to hold back any expectations, yet her

mind kept thinking, *this isn't what I expected.* They had entered the center of the town Waterfield described so vividly. The fountain, the trees, the buildings — all of it stood before her.

Except all of it had died.

The town lay in ruin. The colors of paradise had vanished. An overcast sky lent a gray filter over the place, muting the air with its somber pall. Bare trees and crumbling buildings abound, each one forming its shape through a thin veneer of gray fog like shadow puppets. A chill wind picked up dead leaves and spread them across the chapped ground like a careless vagrant. Even the once beautiful fountain had been toppled over, and the stagnant water in its basin smelled foul.

Elliot let go of Roni's hand as he walked further. She looked in the windows and down a few alleys, but she did not see signs of people. Not even a sound. Only the clinking of their chain.

She glanced back to see the chain stretching right into a ragged opening in the air as if a child had cut out part of the world with dull scissors. Inside the opening, Roni could see the forms of Gram and Sully but as if viewing them through gauze.

Turning back, she walked further into the town. One house, its front door hanging askew, caught Roni's attention — it looked official with two pillars out front and papers attached to a board standing to the side. Symbols on the papers did not match any language she knew. As Elliot came up behind, he pointed to one paper with the writing in large, bold script.

"It is a command to evacuate the town," he said.

"You can read it?"

"I spent a long time here once." He rubbed his eyes and sniffled. "I learned the language."

"Does it say why they had to evacuate? Where they went? Do they give anything to say what happened here?"

"No. And it would not. The people of this world would simply gather their things and start walking until they reached another town."

"And the other town would take them in?"

Elliot's voice cracked. "They were good like that." His legs wobbled and he lowered to the base of the nearest pillar. With his head in his hands, he tears flooded and his shoulders shook.

Roni stood next to him. While she waited, she gazed at the ghost town. In particular, she looked at the dusty ground. Stones of various shapes and sizes littered the area. Which ones were kyolo stones?

After several minutes, Elliot showed no sign of calming down. Roni rubbed her hand along the back of his shoulders. "It'll be okay," she said. "I'm sure they followed the evacuation order."

"I doubt it." He dabbed at his eyes, his voice shaking, and he forced a long inhalation. "I said that the people of this world would pack up and go, but not the people of this town. They were different. They put their souls into making this place as perfect as they could. I don't see how any of them would leave."

"Something bad must've been coming. A plague, maybe, or a terrible storm."

"They would have stayed. They would have faced whatever calamity came their way." Using his cane, he stood. "Do you understand? They stayed, and they stood their ground."

Roni's eyes widened. "And they lost."

"Yes."

"The whole town?"

"It appears so."

"I'm so sorry," she said. She lifted the end of the chain and yanked three times on it — that would appease Gram for five minutes. "What do these kyolo stones look like? I was told they're everywhere."

Elliot paused with a disapproving glare.

"What?" she said. "I came here to fulfill a mission."

"And you found something else. We cannot ignore the tragedy that happened here."

"I'm not suggesting we do. But we should grab the stones we need first. That's our main reason for being in this place."

"Only for you. And you know that to be the case. You know that I came for other reasons, yet you never once bothered to ask me why I want to be here."

Roni's face flushed. "I was being respectful of your privacy."

"You did not want to burden yourself with the concerns of others. You think I do not see what you have become this last year? Sully and I have ears. We have eyes. You think that we did not notice how all of our breakfasts helped you avoid your grandmother? After all, when you and Gram fight in the bookstore, we know it."

Trying to hold back her desire to scream at him, to tell him that she had spoken the truth, that she respected him and that it hurt to think he doubted her sincerity, she gritted her teeth. Because no matter how much truth she spoke, he also spoke the truth. Attempting a calmer tone, she said, "We're here now, and we're alone. Please, tell me what happened."

Elliot leaned on his cane and squinted into the fog. "Do you remember my wife at all?"

"Of course. I loved Auntie Janwan." An image flashed in Roni's mind — Auntie Janwan standing in a kitchen, her body firm and strong, her dark skin glistening with the summer heat. She was baking cookies and she coated the whole house in a sweet, lovely aroma. "She made the best lemon snaps."

Rubbing his belly, he said, "I must have lost twenty pounds after she died."

"It was cancer, right?"

Elliot kicked at the ground. He eyed her as if she had said something profound. "Pancreatic cancer — that was the story we told everybody, but not the entire truth. The real reason she died was because she was a living relic in our world."

Roni glanced at the town buildings. "Auntie Janwan came from here?"

"Oh, yes. This land and our world are closely compatible, but it turns out, that after decades of exposure, her system finally overloaded and shut down."

"Another lie." Her face scrunched as she held back her tears. "She was one of the few memories I could trust, and now you're telling me it was all a lie."

Elliot's hand snapped out fast, smacking Roni upside the head. "Do not ever call my wife *a lie*. She was one of the most beautiful creatures in any world — inside and out. And she loved you. Are you still so childish that you cannot understand the need to perpetuate an untruth when we must protect the secrets of the Parallel Society?"

"Of course not. I'm sorry. It was just a gut reaction. I didn't mean it like it came out."

"Pay attention and maybe you will learn." Rolling his shoulders, he pressed more onto his cane as if he needed it to help him hold the weight of his memory. "When I was thirty-four — which seems like lifetimes ago — back then, I was impulsive and a bit reckless. I had yet to learn more than a few simple tricks I could perform and a few general healing principles, but I thought I had harnessed the greatest forces of the universe. I had not been with the Society long, yet each day brought such wonder and excitement that I grew impatient to learn more. And of course, like you, I was kept away from all the action that I was sure went on without me. Gram had me taking care of the bookstore's ledgers while I also helped keep guard over her office and Sully's workshop. You can imagine how I felt about bookkeeping and guard duty.

"I complained to your grandmother once. After she lectured me for an hour, she showed me the Grand Library. We had a librarian back then — Lydia Schuck — and I was permitted to check out one book at a time. A few months in and I discovered Gerald Waterfield's journal. His descriptions of this paradise world would not leave my mind. Our world was no Utopia, especially for a black man, yet in this journal I read of a world that sounded unreal to me. Unreal and wonderful."

"Yet you went, so part of you must've believed it was real."

"Certainly. According to Gram, no book that makes it into the Grand Library can contain lies. So, I began stocking supplies and a year later, I was ready. My night finally arrived, and I waited for Sully and Gram to go to sleep. Then I snuck into the caverns and used Waterfield's maps to find my way here. When I entered the book, I saw a paradise that made Waterfield's descriptions no more than a braggart's poor rendition of another man's achievements. I could describe this place for months, and still, I would not adequately convey to you the incredible, unimpeachable beauty this world possessed."

Elliot shuffled several steps over. "That fountain was the heart of the town, pumping life into every moment. Its waters could heal people, and it radiated an energy that people craved. An energy of love and kindness. Every town in this world has such a fountain, and as a result, they did not have wars or power grabs or oppressive regimes."

Roni could see that Elliot had become lost in a memory, but she also had an uneasy sensation crawling along her arms — as if someone spied on them. She wanted to get her kyolo stones and leave. "Is that when you met Janwan?"

"Right over there. Next to the fountain. She was with some of her friends, laughing and smiling, and I was taken. I ended up spending the next year here — falling in love and earning her love."

The air around them shifted, and Roni's nerves spiked. She heard something. An animal, perhaps, only it sounded unlike any animal she knew — a throaty breath like a stallion forcing air through its nose followed by a series of clicks.

As she scanned the gray surfaces surrounding them, she said, "Please tell me you know what that was."

Elliot gripped his cane in both hands like a warrior's staff. "I have never heard that sound before."

"We should go."

"Not until we learn what happened here."

Again that horrible combination of breath and clicks.

Roni edged towards the opening that led back to Gram. But if she jumped back in there, Elliot would be left alone. She edge closer to Elliot. But if she stayed, she had no special powers to help him. She would be in the way.

"Please," she said. "We have to go. If you must come back, we can regroup and come in with some sort of plan."

Strong legs thumped against the ground in the distance — a lot of strong legs. Elliot stepped forward, towards the fountain, towards the sound.

Roni grabbed the chain connected to him and yanked him back a step. "You can't go that way. It's my life you're risking, too. Now, help me pick up a few kyolo stones, and then we're leaving."

"We have to know what happened."

"Whatever's out there making that sound, that's what happened."

Elliot's eyes closed as he offered a single, gentle nod. "You are right. You need the kyolo stones. They are smooth and crimson." He smiled at a memory. "They always make me think of gumdrops."

"Where do we find them?"

"Probably at your feet."

Roni gazed down. Numerous stones covered the ground. But all were gray. She bent down and touched one smooth looking stone — gray dust bunched into a small pile as her finger pushed it aside. Underneath, she saw the dark red coloring. Snatching it up, she held it between her thumb and forefinger. "Is this one?"

"Yes," Elliot said. "That is exactly what you seek."

Sweeping her hand in a wide arc across the ground, she discovered over a dozen kyolo stones mixed in with pebbles, rocks, and a few stones of varying colors. She picked out seven kyolo stones and placed them in a small pouch that tied to her belt loop. Her body relaxed slightly — she had succeeded. When they got back to the bookstore, she would contact Kenneth Bay, deliver the stones, and find out how to use them to recover her Lost Time. It had been a difficult trek, but feeling the stones bumping against her thigh made it worthwhile.

Standing, she said, "Okay, let's go back and ..."

Elliot walked away from her — his end of the chain unclipped and dragging behind him like a metallic tail.

"Sonuvabitch," she muttered. Grabbing the chain around her waist, she yanked on it three times. Then she unclipped it, letting it clatter on the ground. Five minutes.

She could get him back before then. Even if she had to knock him in the head to do it.

With fists clenched, she followed him down a street lined with cracked lamps. He halted in front of a fallen tree blocking his way. The top of it had smashed through the window of a two-story home. When he turned around and spied her, he scowled.

"You have your stones. Go back to Gram and Sully."

"I'm not leaving you here."

"You can all come back for me in a few days. I will be fine."

Answering his statement, the deep breath and the rapid clicks. Roni marched down the street with her hand extended. "Don't mess around. Come on. Time to go."

"You are not my mother."

"I'll be a police officer in a second if you don't get moving. I'll bend your arm behind your back and break it, if you make me."

Elliot raised his cane. "Do you really think you have the ability to stop me? Go back to Gram. She knows the rest of my story. She will know what to do for me."

Roni stopped in the middle of the street. Elliot was right, of course — she could not follow through on her threat. She had no special powers. Elliot would never hurt her, but if he was determined to stay in this universe — and clearly, he was — then she could not stop him.

"Please," she said, throwing on a puppy dog look that had always melted his heart when she was a child. "I need you."

"Nothing bad is going to happen to me. I promise I will return. In fact, when I get back, I will explain to you why ..."

His voice trailed off as his gaze lifted from her face to something behind her. Her muscles locked and her pulse quickened. She could feel its presence looming over her. The fear registered on Elliot's face which caused Roni's stomach to knot. And then she heard it — the throaty breath and the hard clicks.

# CHAPTER 14

Roni turned around like a windup toy running low on power. Her arms hung out but they barely moved. Her fingers had locked spread apart. Her eyes refused to blink.

The creature clung sideways to a lamppost. About the size of Roni's torso, it looked like a late day shadow — grayish-black with a soft, uneven outline. It had numerous legs, at least six, but such details were difficult to discern. The creature looked out-of-focus. She could see the way its body segmented like an insect, the way the lower-body had more hair, the way the upper-body looked hard like a carapace, the way its head combined both hair and shell. And its eyes — beads of red shimmering behind the filter that surrounded the creature.

Roni knew exactly what she looked at. The legs, the black hair, the shape of its lower- and upper-body, the demon-like eyes — it all added up to one horrendous name.

*Hellspider.*

"Walk to me," Elliot said, barely above a whisper. "Slowly."

Roni moved her left foot back, and the hellspider

opened its mouth, bared its needle-teeth, and growl-hissed at her. She did not move the right.

"It is okay," Elliot said.

She could hear him moving his arms and pictured him holding his cane up as he prescribed a spell through the air. But a new sound broke her growing hope. Off to the left, a second hellspider clattered over a pile of brick rubble. Another set of clicks announced the arrival of a third hellspider. This one maneuvered along a wall until it looked down from the second floor.

"Elliot? Are you ready yet?" she said.

"I am trying, but I need more time."

"We don't have it." With hellspiders on three sides and a fallen tree behind them, they were pinned. Roni guessed that the creatures had not attacked yet only because they were not sure what to make of Elliot's hand motions. But that caution would not last long. "Forget the spell right now. We've got to get somewhere safe."

The first hellspider once more growl-hissed. The other two launched towards Roni. Without thought, she dropped to the ground. Not a good move. The two hellspiders fell upon her. Every part of her body ignited as the creatures pummeled her with their legs.

But it only lasted seconds.

She heard Elliot grunting, and looking upward, she saw that one hellspider had been thrown back into the rubble pile. Elliot smashed the end of his cane into the second creature.

"Stand," he said.

Roni clambered to her feet as the lead hellspider lowered from the lamppost. Elliot grabbed Roni's hand and guided her toward the nearest doorway — a house on their right. The hellspiders rushed behind their leader, and all three approached. But they did not attack. Cocking their heads, their eyes followed Elliot's cane as he waved it left and right.

Edging toward the door, he said, "When we get inside, run for the back exit. And pray there is one."

Roni opened the door and inched into the entrance. She moved aside and watched as Elliot cleared the jamb. Not waiting for his command, she slammed the door shut. Through small windows at the side, Roni saw the hellspiders jump at the loud bang of the door. She raced down the hallway, following Elliot through a kitchen and toward the back door. They hurtled over a few wooden stairs, crossed a backyard, down an alley, and emerged on another town street.

Waving with one hand, Elliot said, "This way."

Roni hurried to catch up. They jogged across the street and up several blocks. At each corner, Elliot peeked around the edge before leading them further along. When they reached a building that poked outward into the street like an overstuffed belly, Elliot stopped. He touched the building at a spot near his knee, and a round door slid aside.

"Go in," he said.

Roni ducked as she entered. Once inside, Elliot sealed the door with the touch of another unseen button. They were in a store — Roni could tell that much — but the grime-covered windows let only dim light through. A stench of rot permeated the air.

"Into the back," he said.

She kept close as he led the way through an aisle of boxed goods — smiling faces on brightly colored cardboard, each mouth ready to devour bowls of food. Crossing to another aisle, she saw open tables with mounds of rotted and molding fruits. At least, she thought they were fruits. The label did not matter. She had seen enough to confirm they were in a grocery.

When they reached the back of the building, Elliot pressed himself into a corner. "I will get us out of here safely, but you must make sure I have time to do so. Can you do that?"

"I don't really have a choice."

"Not if you want to live."

In his right hand, Elliot held his cane at a slight angle. With his left, he traced a complicated pattern in the air. Roni could not follow all the movements, but the sharp downward motion that began it repeated several times. She wanted to ask him how long he needed, but she also knew better than to interrupt — doing so would only require him to start over.

*Guess I'll defend him until this works. Or I die. One or the other.*

She needed a weapon. Rushing along the back of the store, she glanced up each aisle. At the end, she discovered the source of the horrible stench — the corpse of a rotund person, half their belly excavated by bugs and animals. A shelf had collapsed, much of it leaning on the body, pushing more of its foulness into the air. But on the far side of the mottle-skinned form, she saw something that made her want to scream in frustration — a metal pole. A weapon. Sticking out from the darkness beneath the shelves.

She looked back at Elliot. Maybe she could find a knife or something equally sharp. No. She wouldn't last ten seconds fighting hellspiders with a knife. But that pole would give her distance.

Gripping the shelf, she tried to lift it. No luck. It had been bent and wedged in where it fell. She tried to think of another way to move it, but she had to assume the hellspiders would be upon them any moment. No time to be squeamish.

She rolled her lips into her clamped mouth and held her

breath. Squatting next to the body, she cringed as she reached over the decomposing flesh. Her finger graced the edge of the pole, but she could not snag it.

"Shit." She got on her knees, swallowed down the urge to vomit, and pressed against the corpse until she could grab the pole. With the metal in her hands, she shot back away and stumbled into a display of crunchy food in burlap-type sacks.

The reek wafted over with her, but at least she had the pole. About three feet long, it must have been used to keep the shelf up. Long enough to give her some room to fight. It didn't weigh much, but banging it on the floor showed her it could take a few hits and not bend.

She rushed back to Elliot. Though his eyes had closed, he continued motioning through the air around his cane — never once accidentally bumping it. When she was a teenager, she once walked into his apartment while he meditated. He took no notice of her, so she stood in the doorway and watched him for a while. The serene look on his face at that time left her feeling the same — calm and at peace.

Sitting in the back of a grocery, Elliot displayed none of that ease. His brow wrinkled as he concentrated, and his motions lacked all the peaceful grace that teenage girl once saw. Elliot was worried and trying hard to finish before the hellspiders arrived.

But he could not rush those hands or the results. Planting the end of the pole down, Roni stood a few feet in front of him, and she waited. *I am the last line of defense.*

More accurately, she was the only line of defense.

A loud whine of metal from the front reverberated throughout the store. She gripped the pole in both hands and crouched in a stance she hoped would be good for fighting. Three bangs followed, and the door careened into the store, smashing through several shelves of glass items. They shattered, riddling the floor with tiny shards that tinkled like a chandelier.

Then Roni heard it. Deep, throaty breath. Rapid clicks.

In the dim light, she found it difficult to make out the details of the far aisles. She had to assume that at least one hellspider would come from there — thought she could hear it, too. She caught sight of another as it vaulted atop the shelves and gazed down at her. And the third?

She heard it charge from her left side. She had thought she could see that side fine, but what she mistook for a shadow now moved like a stampeding bull. Jumping back, she swung the pole and clocked the hellspider in the side of the head — all luck, but it worked. The hellspider slid across the floor and smacked against the wall. Though still conscious, it wobbled as it struggled to stand again.

The other two growl-hissed as they took the offensive. Roni whirled back, letting the pole take the lead. The hellspider from above dodged her attack and regrouped at her left flank. Watching it carefully, she heard the other one too late. From out of the dark, it launched towards her. Two shadowy legs bashed against her — one connecting with her hip, the other knocking her in the head.

She dropped to the floor. The metal pole clanged and rolled away. Rubbing her temple, she tried to sit up, but another shadowy limb slammed into her side. She fell to the floor.

From her back, she lifted her head. All three hellspiders closed in. They opened their greedy mouths. Saliva dribbled off their teeth. They were hungry.

Roni thought of the corpse on the other side of the store. These things had eaten everyone — or at least, the parts they wanted. Roni and Elliot were warm, fresh meat.

The lead hellspider reared back on four legs and jumped

into the air. Roni thrust her arm up as if she could stop the attack. To her shock, the hellspider froze in the air. It hovered above her, wiggling its legs without effect. Then it slid in an arc downward to the ground as if stuck on the outside of a glass dome.

*A dome?*

She looked behind her. Elliot stood with his cane held high above his head and his left hand glowing pale red. His arms shook with effort and his face betrayed the deep concentration he exerted. Roni had a million questions flooding her mind, but survival instincts kicked in.

She jumped to her feet. "Can we leave now?"

Elliot walked forward, and Roni stayed close by his side. As they moved, the invisible dome moved with them, pushing the hellspiders back. Growl-hissing erupted from the three creatures, but they retreated each time Elliot stepped ahead. Though slow-going, Roni moved at Elliot's pace.

Proceeding up one aisle, the field around them shoved boxes aside. Even the shelving bowed away from them. When they reached the exit — now a ragged hole where the entranceway had been — Elliot turned back to face the hellspiders. Two of the creatures shot forward and rammed the dome. They only succeeded in bruising their heads.

"Outside," Elliot said, his voice strained.

Roni obeyed. When she stepped onto the sidewalk, she felt a warm tingling as she walked through the dome. Looking back, Elliot had one foot on the wall and the other in the store. Easing backwards, he ducked. His hands stretched forward, and the tip of his cane still worked inside the store.

"Be ready," he said.

*Ready for what?*

Motioning a different pattern in the air, Elliot scurried

backwards in her direction. His hand still glowed, but the light dimmed. As he came near her, the hellspiders made more noise before crawling through to the sidewalk.

Roni finally saw it all — like an open umbrella the dome would not fit through the opening in the wall. Elliot had to get Roni out and then himself before he could contract its area of effectiveness. Now, with the closed dome in his hand, the hellspiders moved freely. They bolted toward Roni, but Elliot had already reached her. He opened his palm, spun his hand in the air, and she heard a sizzle as the dome reformed around them.

But Elliot stumbled into her arms. Sweat soaked his brow. The hellspiders scratched at the dome, growl-hissed at it, and paced around its perimeter. Though they could not find a way in, they seemed to understand that Elliot would not be able to hold the dome forever.

"Come on," Roni said, ducking under the arm that held his cane. "Lean your weight on me, and we'll get back to Gram and Sully."

Limping up the street, Roni guided Elliot toward the opening to the book and the caverns. They had to go around the block. Having seen the difficulty Elliot faced getting them safely out of the store, Roni thought it best to avoid passing through the house again.

The hellspiders never let up their attacks. Either the creatures weren't too bright and thought they could muscle their way through the dome, or they were smarter than expected and they were testing for weakness. Or they were starving.

One other possibility came to mind, and it bothered Roni the most — the hellspiders might be attacking simply to keep the pressure on. To intimidate.

As they turned the corner, all thoughts of hellspiders vanished. Roni stumbled, nearly fell to her knees, as she stared at the empty street. How long had they been? Certainly more than five minutes. But the idea that Gram would truly reel in her chain, that she would close the book, that any part of her could sacrifice her own granddaughter — Roni's mind went numb.

Elliot shoved her as he moved ahead. "Get to the pathway."

"What pathway?"

"The gash floating in the air — our way back through the book."

Of course. The book was still open. Roni could see the opening in the air — the pathway. Hobbling onward, they reached the halfway point in the street, when the pathway shimmered as if behind a clear waterfall.

Her heart jolted. Was that what it looked like when a book closed?

But a figure stepped through. A boxy, stout figure with a large chest and a stern, determined expression — Gram. She had a chain crossing over her front to form an X. It stretched back through the pathway, presumably to Sully. As Gram took in her surroundings, the hellspiders stopped attacking the dome.

Before Roni could think what to do, her instincts kicked into action. She burst through the warm tingle of the dome and sprinted towards Gram. "Go back!"

Gram smiled at her, but the smile faded fast. Roni didn't need to hear the growl-hisses and the thundering of twenty-some feet chasing behind her. Waving for Gram to turn back, she pressed onward.

But Gram did not listen. She released a new chain from her sleeve and spun it over her head like a cowboy preparing to lasso a calf. Her eyes locked just behind Roni.

*It might work.* If Roni could run straight by Gram, the hellspiders would follow. Gram could strike with her chain, whip it across all three, and hopefully injure them enough for Elliot to make it to the pathway. Yes, Roni could see it all happen as if they had planned it that way all along.

Then Roni tripped.

She hit the ground hard, rocks and dirt finding their way beneath her damp clothes as she tumbled forward. The hellspiders raced by her, but two of them made tight arcs and curved back. The lead hellspider continued after Gram.

Tasting blood on her lips, Roni rolled onto her feet. With one hellspider on either side and no metal pole in hand, she did not see how to get free. From the corner of her eye, she caught sight of Elliot, but he was too far away to rescue her. Gram had a hellspider of her own to contend with.

Roni's right leg shivered. Her left fingers tapped. Her heart raced.

She never saw the signal, yet both hellspiders lunged after her simultaneously. Her fingers curled into fists. She had no expectation of defeating them, not dealing with both at once, but she hoped to get a couple of solid punches in first.

Right before she pulled back her arm to strike, she heard Elliot scream as if far away. Thinking of him falling under those tooth-riddled mouths angered her more. She roared and swung her fist.

But she never had time to connect.

A single pulse of sound erupted like a flash of lightning. A sound thick as clay, sharp as razor. It shook Roni's limbs, shuddered her muscles, jarred her teeth. Though it lasted less than a second, she covered her ears and dropped to her knees. The ground lifted beneath her as she lost all sense of balance. With her cheek pressed into the dirt, she saw that the hellspiders had suffered even worse — one stumbled like a drunk, another lay on its back wriggling, and the third dragged itself using only three legs.

She heard nothing.

All sounds had fallen away. Not even a ringing in her ears. Simply silence.

She rolled onto her back. Gram crawled on all fours. It seemed she tried to get near Roni, but her disorientation had her weaving away as much as towards her granddaughter.

Roni attempted sitting up but only succeeded in flopping onto her side once again. Her new angle gave her a view of Elliot. She had to be hallucinating — Elliot stood firm and unaffected.

He surveyed the scene, dropped to his knees, and dug into the ground. Roni reached out to him — tried to, but her hand fell to the ground. He pulled something from his shirt and buried it. Rubbing his face — *tears?* — he stood. She tried to call him but could not make a sound.

Working hard with his cane, he managed to move closer towards her. Agonizing step after agonizing step. The pain wrinkling his brow, the sweat dripping off his chin, and the blood dribbling from his nose all told Roni that she did not hallucinate. Elliot must have created a hellish force.

She tried to smile — *a hellish force for a hellish spider.*

When he finally reached her, he bent down and clipped the end of his chain to one that Gram had tossed across the ground. Roni could not recall when Gram had done so, but there the chain waited. He then tied an end around her waist and secured it.

"Now, Lillian," he said, though Roni only saw his lips move.

Though Gram still weaved and wobbled, she had enough control to grab onto the chain and tug it repeatedly. Seconds later, the chain reeled into the pathway. In another universe, Sully had to be digging his feet in hard as he pulled all three of his friends back to safety.

Roni had the barest awareness of dragging along the ground. When she slipped out of the book and onto the sand of the Isle, her imbalance helped her a bit — just another disorientation. The change in the way the air smelled, however, woke her senses faster.

Her hearing returned to the level of a muted undersea sound, but it was enough. She heard Gram yelling, "We're through. We're through. Close it."

Sully dropped the chains and hustled over to the book. He snapped the cover shut before a single hellspider could escape.

# CHAPTER 15

Roni kept her eyes closed, feeling the cool grains of sand along the back of her neck, beneath her fingers, and under her legs. She wanted to move and not to move. If she kept her eyes closed, she could be at the beach hearing the soft waves under the cool night stars. But she heard Gram to her left sitting up, and to her right, Sully helped Elliot do the same.

"Is everyone okay?" Elliot asked.

Roni heard Gram brushing sand off her clothes as she stood. There would be no reprieve. Roni opened her eyes. "I'm okay. What did you do to us?"

Elliot sat with his bare feet in the sand. While Sully knelt behind him and massaged his temples, Elliot said, "I used the power that I had hoped I never would have to use. I learned of it in one of the old journals in the Grand Library. You see, you are not the only one who ever steps foot in there."

"We've all made use of the Library, too," Gram said as she walked over to the book. With a practiced hand, she created chains and wrapped them around the cover like ribbons around a Christmas present. "I'd still like an answer to Roni's question, though. I've never seen you do that before. I'd like to know if there's going to be some residual effects. Like this ringing in my ear — how long is that going to last?"

"There has been no permanent damage, I promise you. As to the reason why you have never seen me do this before, it is because creating that particular shockwave, the kind that disoriented those creatures, puts great strain upon me."

Sully said, "He's underselling it. The words *great strain* mean it damn near killed him. Maybe when he was a younger man, but at our age, he shouldn't be creating that kind of thing."

"It was, as you have probably begun to surmise, a loud blast of sound. It self–calibrated to cause maximum damage to those creatures while harming us the least possible."

"That was the least possible?" Gram said. "I'll pray we never have to experience it again."

Elliot leaned over towards his side. Sully held him as his stomach convulsed. But after three fruitless heaves, Elliot continued down until his cheek rested firmly in the sand.

Roni had made it to her feet. "Any idea how long it'll take him to recover?"

"What's the rush?" Sully said. "You have somewhere special to be?"

"Sorry, no. I'm just happy to be done with this. We have a long walk home, and I'm looking forward to a hot bath. That's all."

Gram crouched near the pedestal, poking at a hole in the sand. "We're not leaving yet."

"I got the kyolo stones, so the mission is over. It's what we came for. Of course, we'll wait for Elliot to feel better, but —"

"I'm not talking about Elliot." She looked to Sully. "I'm

sure he'll be fine. In fact, we need him to be fine. Look at these marks."

Roni did not need to inspect the holes that had caught Gram's interest. She already knew. "It's another hellspider, isn't it?"

"I'm afraid so. From these marks, I'm guessing it's a much larger version. You said you saw something when we were on the river, and we all saw the dead relics and the missing books. And now these footprints. When I went in that book to get you out, I saw what those creatures had done to the place. We can't let that thing remain free in these caverns."

Sully said, "Of course not."

Roni spit sand off her lips. "Are you losing your mind in your old age? Elliot and I barely survived fighting off those hellspiders. You didn't fare much better. And now look at him. He can't even sit up. There is no way we can go fighting a mama hellspider without Elliot, and he's in no shape to do anything."

Brushing off her hands, Gram walked toward the raft. "Elliot can rest in here while we paddle. If we move the supplies around, he'll fit. It might be a little scrunched for us, but we'll manage."

"Listen to me. We are too weak to take this thing on." Roni wanted to mention her father's warnings, but she held back. Gram had already made up her mind and mentioning the ravings of a man in a mental hospital would only stir her anger. Roni had enough anger for the both of them. She figured if she got Gram equally upset, they might cause a seismic event.

"Dear, I'm not a fool. I know what we are facing."

"Then why —"

"We are talking about entire universes. Each book out there represents billions, maybe trillions or quadrillions, of lives. Probably even more. Infinite lives. You were in that world, you saw what the hellspiders did. How many universes is enough before we act?"

"I'm not saying we should allow the hellspider to go destroying universes. But running into a fight down a man — particularly, the only one of us who has managed to stop these things — it seems a bit idiotic."

"We don't have a choice. This is the job."

"I thought the job was to protect our own universe, and we can't do that if we all end up dead."

Gram tilted her head with an understanding grin. "I know this is scary. I'm at the end of my life as it is, and Lord knows, I'm terrified. But what do you think happens if we allow this cavern, this incredible and impossible cavern, what do you think happens to our world if this place is destroyed? Come now, I know you. You are not a heartless person. Rather than fighting me on this decision, you should be helping me figure out how to make it work."

With his head still against the sand, Elliot said, "May I weigh in on this?" Using Sully to assist, he managed to get into a sitting position. "Roni seems to have forgotten that I am a healer. It will not take me long to be ready."

"You see? He's going to be fine."

"I did not say that. I will be ready, but there are limits to how much healing I can do to myself, even under the best of circumstances. And even if I were to be as strong as I was twenty years ago, do not expect me to use that sound blast again."

Sully approached the raft and wagged his finger. "He's got you there. Both of you are right and both of you are wrong. With an answer like that, Elliot would make a good Rabbi."

Though she smirked, Gram said, "Right or wrong, I'm still the leader of this group. So, let's get this raft ready.

Elliot, you rest. When the time comes, we'll need you to do everything you can."

Straightening her back as if she tried to grow a few inches, she stared at Roni. For a moment, Roni's chest withered as it had so many times when she was younger and had to endure her grandmother drawing a line in the sand. But this situation was different. She was no longer a little girl who had made a mistake. In fact, she knew she was right. She understood Gram's position, but a leader had to make tough choices — and in this case, the decision was between losing several universes while they regained their strength versus fighting now, losing, and watching *all* the universes be destroyed. She wondered if Gram sought to go out in a blaze. Unfortunately, Roni also recognized that the Old Gang would stick together. She could not let them face the hellspider alone. So, doing her best to avoid meeting Gram's eyes, Roni helped Sully prepare the raft.

By the time they were ready, Elliot had managed to stand with the aid of his cane. Gram walked him to the edge of the water, and Sully assisted him into the raft. After a little finagling, they all managed to find a space, gather their oars, and push off onto the lake.

Roni watched the sands of the Isle recede and wondered if all her experiences with the books in the cavern would be like this. Every book she had encountered led to horror. Even the one that had promised to be a paradise — it came the closest to killing her. The whole world had become like that. On the surface, the world offered opportunity and a chance for happiness. But beneath the façade resided an ugly truth. The world was like all the others out there. It promised one thing and delivered another. It was a fairytale — on the surface a pleasant children's story, but beneath, a dark and sinister gaze into the abyss of mankind's heart.

And yet she still wanted to save it.

Perhaps it was Waterfield's journal. Perhaps it was seeing the way Elliot and Sully and even Gram fought for it. Perhaps it was nothing more than the survival instinct. Whatever the case, deep in her core, she would continue to fight for their world. Having learned the truth and joined the Parallel Society, she felt a duty, if not an honor, to fulfill this task.

But Gram was wrong. Her decision would most likely cost the lives of many universes and that might include their own. Roni wanted to take over, but she doubted Sully and Elliot would follow her. They trusted her well enough, but after decades of being part of the Old Gang, their allegiance went to Gram. Understandable, but frustrating.

"To the left," Gram said, pointing toward a rocky ledge poking out over the water.

Working together, they maneuvered the raft to the ledge, so that Gram could safely step out and tie them off. Getting Elliot onto the ledge proved more difficult. But they managed.

They could only walk single file down the narrow tunnel. Gram led the way with her flashlight while Sully brought up the rear. Elliot managed a slow pace using his cane in the right hand and the wall on his left side. Behind him, Roni stayed ready in case she needed to catch him should he fall.

"If you want to take a rest," Roni said, "just say the word."

Breathing heavily with a wheeze when he inhaled, Elliot gave a slight nod.

Sully said, "Quit worrying about him. He's been in great shape his whole life. I'm the one that needs your concern."

Roni looked back to wink when she noticed that the tunnel receded into darkness. She had not realized they had come so far. Only a few minutes later, the rocky walls smoothed out. Several steps after that, they became tiled walls like an old New York City subway.

"Are we in another universe?" Roni asked.

"Very possible," Gram said, flashing her light over the group. "Often a change like this indicates a new universe. But nothing is a guarantee."

The tunnel continued straight onward, never once curving left or right. Though not prone to claustrophobia, Roni found the cramped quarters disturbing. She kept thinking that should the hellspider attack now, they would be helpless. Yet Gram pushed forward. She seemed to quicken their pace, pushing them as fast as Elliot could handle. Roni wanted to say something, wanted to scold the woman for having no compassion, but anything that slowed them down meant they would spend that much longer as easy targets in this awful tunnel.

As if treating her thoughts like prayers, they came to a crossroads. The corners between each tunnel had been flattened, and a bench had been carved into the stone. Above each bench, a carved face gazed down. Not human faces. Nor animal. Rather, they were in amalgamation of both that left Roni with a disquieted sensation roiling in her gut.

Gram pointed to one bench. "Have a seat. Let's rest and figure out which way to go."

Elliot plopped down. The collar of his shirt had warped loose with sweat. As Sully peered into each tunnel, Roni sat next to Elliot and held his hand. His fingers would not be still — they danced against her while his other hand gripped his cane as if it were a life preserver. To see this man who had always been a paragon of health tremble before her churned her thoughts into a dark future — the reality that Death waited for the Old Gang. While everybody faced dying eventually, the strain on Elliot made his passing more concrete, more certain.

"He can't go on like this," Roni said.

Leaning forward while attempting to smile, Elliot said, "I am fine. Just a little winded. It is not easy hiking day after day, not at my age."

Gram crossed her arms and gazed down to appraise him. "You know what we've got to do. I'm trusting you to tell me if you're not up to the task."

"I have always been up to the task."

Roni looked between the two as if watching insane people self-diagnose. "Look at him. What part of him looks ready to take on a hellspider? Is it the way he can hardly breathe? Or perhaps you find his sweat-stained clothes more convincing?"

Elliot raised his shaking hand to quell any further arguments. Leveling a firm stare at Roni, he said, "Our job is not to live forever. We are here to fight, to protect our universe. We are sentinels, guardians, soldiers. You have to accept a lot of hard truths in order to be an effective member of the Parallel Society. Please, do not make them harder for me, Gram, or Sully."

Despite his conviction and sincerity, Roni could not believe all that Elliot had said. She suspected that at least part of him acted out of loyalty to Gram and nothing more. Yet despite her misgivings, she backed off. Outnumbered in this debate and outmaneuvered by Elliot, she had no choice but acceptance — after all, she still needed them to guide her back home.

Even as she nodded her acquiescence, she crossed to the opposite bench. With a silent vow, she decided that upon their return, she would rely only upon herself. Maybe someday she could have a team like the Old Gang, but until that day, the universe would still need protection. And these old folks seemed determined to kill themselves.

Gram stroked Elliot's cheek. "You are sure you can

handle this?"

Roni huffed. "Now you suddenly care?"

Gram did not bother to look back. "Before, you said you could not find this creature. Won't it still be that hard?"

Elliot raised his cane and hand. "At that time, I did not know what I sought. But I have faced these creatures now. It will still be difficult here in the caverns, but I believe I can manage. And besides, after all this arguing, it would be a waste not to try."

For ten excruciating minutes, Roni sat on her bench, arms folded, and watched Elliot strain through his motions in order to locate the hellspider. She could not decide what she hated more — her inability to prevent this, Gram's willingness to push Elliot, or the way Sully had remained silent throughout the entire debate. The stone faces above mocked her like a group of adults gazing down at a foolish child.

As if bursting into the air from beneath the ocean, Elliot gasped. He dropped his cane and slumped back against the stone wall. Sully raced to his side. In that instant, Roni saw how the last ten minutes had strained Sully as well.

"Are you okay?" he asked.

Though woozy, Elliot managed to say, "The hellspider can be found at the end of that passageway." He pointed to the West. "Good luck." With nothing more, he passed out.

Sully gazed up at Gram, a mixture of anger and understanding combating upon his features. "I will stay here and watch over him."

There was no room for debate in his tone. Perhaps Gram agreed with him, too. She bent down and picked up the cane with a gentle touch. As she handed it to Sully, she said, "Of course. We can't leave him here alone, and I can think of no better than you to protect him. Roni and I will handle things just fine." She looked at Roni, and with a doubtful expression, she said, "Isn't that right, dear?"

Roni could barely open her tense mouth. "Absolutely."

"Then let's go." As she stepped toward the West passageway, she turned to Sully. "Give us at least a half hour. If we don't come back —"

"No need to finish that," Sully said. "We've been down this road too many times. I know what to do."

Flashing a warm smile, Gram said, "You always make me proud."

As she headed down the tunnel, Roni followed. That final comment buzzed in the air between them like a World War II bomber waiting to drop its payload. Roni had too many emotions juggling within her. In the end, she shoved it all down to be dealt with later. Those bombs had to drop sometime. But for now, they had a hellspider to find.

# CHAPTER 16

For such an old woman, Gram sure could set a strong pace. Though they only had their flashlights to see by, it was enough for Roni to catch the anger in her grandmother. Fine with her. She had just as much anger and more to spare.

Before they had time to boil over, the tunnel ended with a wooden door. Gram inspected the door from top to bottom with her flashlight. She then placed her hand on the wood, followed by an ear. Looking back at Roni, she shook her head. "I'm not picking up anything."

"You have another power?"

"Lord, no. I only mean I don't see anything, I don't feel anything, and I don't hear anything. If it's not safe to open the door, I'm not getting any indication."

"I guess we'll just have to try our luck."

Brushing her sides with her hands, Gram said, "Unless you, perhaps, read something in Waterfield's journal that might help."

Despite all her anger and frustration, part of Roni recognized how difficult it must have been for Gram to admit she needed the expertise of the researcher. It didn't change the overall problems, and it didn't solve their troubles, but Gram's passive admission eased the pressure. Even if only for a little while.

"Waterfield never got this far. Remember, for him, the Book on the Isle led to a paradise. He had no reason to go exploring further. And he lacked the support of his teammates." She hadn't meant to throw that jibe, but once it was out, she could do nothing more about it.

Gram flinched but covered it up by turning to the door. "Then it's like you said. We'll have to take our chances." She reached for the handle.

They walked into a ballroom-sized space with piles of books making mountains along the sides. In the center of the room upon a stone platform awaited a chair carved in stone. Either a throne room or a courtroom — Roni couldn't tell which. The carvings on the walls and the architecture of the platform had a distinct flavor to it — like something dwarves made in a Tolkien novel.

Their footsteps echoed in the open space, and Roni breathed easier now that she had escaped the tunnels. The air smelled stale. Sharp too. Roni thought that odd. Running her flashlight beam across the ground, she discovered the source of the odor — old droppings from above. Arching her ear upward, she listened for the telltale squeaks of bats or batlike creatures. She heard nothing.

"Whatever caused this mess," Gram said, "it happened quite a while ago. You can see how dry it all is. And fresher business doesn't dry out the air."

Roni fought back the urge to throw up. "We're breathing crap?"

"Dear, we've been breathing it for days now. Not a lot of air circulation in these caverns."

Roni clamped her mouth shut. But breathing through her nose only intensified the foul odors. Not breathing seem like a poor choice. She opted to switch back and forth, a few breaths at a time — she would've preferred a gasmask but never saw one in the supplies Sully and Elliot had packed.

Gram played her light over the book piles. "Looks like we found the missing books."

Looking closer, Roni spotted torn chains still hanging from the spines of several books. "Great. We've confirmed that this is where the creature's taking those books, and that means we've done a good job of reconning the situation. Let's go back, get Elliot and Sully, strengthen up, and return here when we're ready to fight."

"Not yet. We only know that this is where the books have been stored. We don't know for sure that your hellspider is what brought them here."

"It is not *my* hellspider."

"I don't see any of those large round marks on the ground. Do you? Anything to indicate the hellspider."

"Are you saying there's some other kind of creature out there that's stealing these books?"

Gram shrugged. "We have to stay open to all the possibilities."

They walked deeper into the room, and Roni sensed greater pressure from the large open space as she neared the chair. *More likely a courtroom,* she thought. Facing judgment while sitting in that chair surrounded by this huge space would be maddening.

Once on the platform, she had no doubt the room had been set up to intimidate. "We shouldn't be here," Roni said.

"Nonsense. We are the Parallel Society. It is our duty to be here."

Roni's skin prickled. She thought she heard something — a rustling of clothes or bristling of hair.

Gram turned in a slow circle. "I don't see any other doors or passageways out besides the one we used. Unless these hellspiders can squish their limbs like an octopus, I don't see how the big one would be able to get through the tunnel."

As the answer hit Roni, so did the sound — a deep breath like a foghorn, rapid clicks like an amplified centipede. All from above. *Oh, shit.* Shrinking under her suspicions, Roni raised her light to the ceiling. Gram's light joined in, and they moved along the uneven surface searching for the source of the noise.

"We should go," Roni said even as she continued searching.

"Not until we're sure."

"We know exactly what's up there."

"Really? Tell me then — is there just one or a hundred up there? We have to know what we're facing. Then we go."

Several feet from the end of the room, they found it.

The hellspider clung to where the wall and ceiling met, blending in with the rocks and crevices formed by the cavern. Too far away for Roni to get a clear idea of its size, she could see enough to be sure of one thing — this one was definitely bigger.

Roni put her mouth to Gram's ear, and softer than before, she said, "We need to leave right now."

Keeping her light on the hellspider, Gram eased back, quiet step by quiet step. Her breathing quickened. Roni followed, her chest tightening until she remembered to breathe. She inhaled with an audible gasp and snapped her hand over her mouth.

With a shaky beam, she brought her light upon the hellspider. Two large, long legs unfolded out of the crevice and clamped onto the ceiling. The creature pushed and emerged from its hole. Hanging upside down, it gazed upon them with horrid red eyes. Roni stood still like a mouse caught between the paws of a cat — knowing it needed to break for freedom but terrified that the cat would pounce.

It held its stare, and she had the passing thought that the hellspider might have been as surprised to see her as she was to see it. However, she did not think any form of amicable understanding crossed between them — indeed, she had the distinct impression that the hellspider was sizing up the form of threat she posed. Still, there was an instant, the briefest of flashes, in which Roni thought perhaps the hellspider decided there was no threat. In that sliver of time, she saw the creature inch back towards its crevice in the ceiling.

But then Gram released one of her chains.

Roni snapped her attention toward the gentle rattle as its echo amplified throughout the room. Gram grabbed the loose end to quiet the noise, but it was too late. The hellspider's limbs stiffened as it cocked its head toward the new sound. It raced across the ceiling, chunks of stone dropping to the ground where it released its footing. In seconds, it had reached the front of the room, crawled down the side, and blocked the only exit.

Gram faced the hellspider, feet in a wide stance like a gunfighter at high noon. The hellspider shifted on its numerous legs and glowered down upon them from its ten foot height. Roni's feet became as solid as the stone around them — she couldn't move.

She had seen monsters before — the creature Darin had become, a giant hand reaching out of a book, and most recently, the three small hellspiders. But she had never set eyes upon such a truly monstrous creature. Its sheer size pulled it out of her memories of scary stories told late at night.

Having so few memories to cling to, she marveled at the idea that this ten foot colossus could bring forward one of the darker images within her. Even as her heart pulsed with uncertainty, another part of her, a part rarely touched upon, sparked. That same part of her hopeful enough to send her into these caverns searching for kyolo stones. That part of her determined to get back to her world so that she could use the stones to unlock her memories — hopefully.

Gram twirled the chain at her side. The hellspider swayed as if locked in strong air currents from its height.

"I don't want to hurt you," Gram said even as she set one foot behind to brace herself. "But you don't belong here. If you let me, I'll help you. If you can show me what book you came from, I'll send you back there. If you don't want that, that's fine, too. There are other worlds I can send you to where you'll do no harm. The choice is yours, but that is the limit of your choice. You do not get to stay here."

If the hellspider understood a single word she spoke, it never showed it. Roni, however, caught Gram's response — a slight drop of her shoulders. Disappointment. Perhaps even a touch of regret. But not enough to stop her from attacking.

Like a stagecoach driver whipping her team of horses into action, Gram snapped out her chain at the hellspider. For one glorious second, Roni saw the future unfold before her. She saw the chain grab into the heart of the creature. She saw how Gram's magic subdued the creature. She saw the strength of her grandmother and the way the old woman never faltered as she sent the hellspider into a book she held.

But that was all in her mind's eye. None of it happened.

As the chain sailed forward, the hellspider moved with

astonishing speed. It snagged the chain out of the air with one leg and took control with two more. Moving with grace and agility, it rolled its body toward the left with a ferocious motion that rippled down the chain. Gram never had time to react.

Power released from the chain, up Gram's arm, and sent her flying across the room. She slammed through a pile of books and crashed to the floor. As the books opened, the mayhem began.

Storms clashed within the room. One book sucked air into it with tremendous force while another blew air out shoving over a pile of books. In front of Roni, an open book spewed out rain and hail into the air with such force that she could hear it rattling upon the ceiling. Another book culled all of that water and ice back into it. Lightning flashed out of one book while the howls of strange creatures echoed from another.

The hellspider worked its way around the raging winds in its effort to reach Gram. Wiping the rainwater from her face, Roni found her legs. She rushed across the room toward her grandmother.

"Close the books!" Gram whipped out chain after chain trying to lock down the open universes.

Roni pivoted to the right and started shutting the covers as she passed them. But for every book she closed, the strong winds knocked open two more.

The hellspider crept along the wall working its way up and over piles of books. It paused to observe Gram's movements. Like an astronaut in zero-gs, the hellspider pushed off the wall and sailed across the air. Roni could see the trajectory. The hellspider would land right beside the stone chair, and it would be in a perfect position to attack Gram.

Flashes of light and heat burst toward her right. An

open book spit out plumes of fire and smoke. Roni leapt over, plucked up the book, and pointed it at the space where she expected the hellspider to drop.

Fire shot out of the book. The cover vibrated in her hands, and the heat built up against her palms. She had a brief moment of satisfaction when she saw understanding cross the red eyes of the hellspider. It knew the trouble it was in.

As it landed in a sea of fire, Roni heard the creature shriek. The sound of its pain brought her own pain to the forefront of her mind. Her hands felt as if they were on fire. She dropped to her knees, determined to keep that book open as long as it took to protect Gram. Tears streamed down her face. She opened her mouth and roared her anguish. Through blurry vision, she finally saw the hellspider escape back up the wall and toward the ceiling.

She dropped the book using her elbows to close the cover.

"That one," Gram said, pointing toward a book that threw large puffy white snowflakes into the air.

Roni scurried toward the book and plunged her hands in between its covers. Cool air and icy flakes soothed her immediately.

Leaning back, Gram's face turned red as she struggled to tighten a chain around one book while a winged-beast flapped and thumped an escape attempt. "When you can hold that book of fire again, let me know. It's all we've got so far that'll work."

Though Roni said nothing, she gaped at her grandmother's cruelty. Knowing the pain Roni had just endured, Gram made no effort to locate a different book to utilize. Or simply let the hellspider go. They did not have their full team, and they had sustained injury. They were in no shape to continue the fight. Besides, the hellspider had been hurt, too. It sat on the wall licking its burns. It showed little interest in them anymore. Yes, they needed to capture it and place it in a book, but Roni thought it would be better to regroup, reorganize, and then return.

Huffing and sweating, Gram tossed aside the latest chained book. She paused to kiss the cross around her neck. "Now, Roni, while we still have a chance."

A ridiculous statements — they had no chance.

The hellspider lumbered across the wall toward the back, hanging above a tall stack of books that had managed to stay standing. Stretching toward the pile with one of its back, singed legs, it snatched a book off the top. With a deft maneuver, it tossed the book into the air and caught it with its front legs. Holding the book out the full length of its legs, the hellspider opened the cover.

A mild breeze puffed out against the dark hairs on its face. It squinted, and for a moment, Roni thought the hellspider would do its work for them. She could see it simply walk into the book and all would be well. But she knew that was nothing more than wishful thinking.

Emitting a deep, grinding noise, the hellspider's neck elongated towards the book. Roni flinched backwards, her hands breaking free from the soothing cold. The creature opened its mouth. And continued opening its mouth, unhinging its jaw like a serpent, until its orifice measured twice the size of its normal head.

While Gram continued to chain down books, Roni watched the creature inhale the air of the book. The wind whipping around the edges of the cover howled like a ghost. The hellspider widened its mouth, and the wind it inhaled strengthened. Roni wanted to ask Gram if she knew what was happening, but she didn't dare turn away.

Another hellspider, this one small like those Roni had fought alongside Elliot, now burst forth through the book and hovered in the air between book and mouth. It lasted only seconds, but Roni swore she saw an odd look on the new hellspider's face — perhaps confusion, perhaps fear. Flailing its many limbs around like a rag doll in a hurricane, it tumbled into the mouth of the larger hellspider.

A snap of the jaw. A snap of the cover. All went quiet.

Lifting one of its burned legs, the hellspider watched as its blistered skin healed. Roni glanced at her own reddened hands — they would take weeks to heal, at least. Though she could not be sure, she swore the hellspider appeared to have grown as well. Not much — perhaps less than an inch — but enough to be noticeable. With its newly healed leg, the hellspider reached down to swipe another book.

"Fuck that," Roni said.

With an enraged war cry, she swept up the fire book and sprinted toward the hellspider. The creature took no notice of her, occupied by its own healing process. She reached the bottom of the pile of books that towered above and began climbing.

Progress slowed as half the books she stepped upon slipped beneath her feet to tumble toward the bottom. Turned out that a pile of books did not create the sturdiest of structures. Too many wobbled like her heart. What began as a bold reaction settled firmer into self-doubt with each step higher. When she passed the halfway point, Roni wondered how much range the fire book needed. The sooner she could open it onto the hellspider, the happier she would be. But her calculations were unnecessary. The hellspider had noticed her.

It scrabbled down the wall and onto the top of the book pile. Roni heard Gram's chains shooting out and wrapping up books as they fell to the ground.

"Come on a little closer," Roni said. "Come on now. I've got a little something for you."

She climbed up another book, and the hellspider reared back, hissing and clicking. Moving sideways like a crab, it dropped down several feet and narrowed its red eyes on the perch beneath Roni's foot.

"Oh. Is one of your friends in there?" Risking a fall that would end her, Roni scrunched down and picked up the book that held the hellspider's interest. It had a green leather cover and weighed more than the fire book.

The hellspider sidestepped again, dropping lower, almost parallel with Roni. Clearly this creature wanted to leap forward and grab the book, but it had learned a healthy appreciation for its foe.

Holding both books, Roni could not decide what to do. Part of her wanted to burn the creature as before. Part of her wanted to burn the green leather book. But as the hellspider inched closer, the answer clarified before her.

Holding up the green book, she said, "You want this? Come and get it."

Like a puppy offered a treat from a stranger, the hellspider approached with its fear and desire fighting out upon its face. Roni watched each footfall. The closer it advanced, the more its massive size loomed over her. Her throat tightened, and she hoped the creature could not sense her deception or worse, her fear.

One more step. That was all she needed. One more step, and she thought the hellspider would be close enough.

"You're acting a little unsure. How about this? How about I set this book down so you can pick it up?" Putting words to action, she placed the green book upon a sturdy section of the pile. Then she backed away a few steps.

The hellspider lurched forward. Its sudden movements sent a mini-avalanche of books tumbling downward to the floor. As it took hold of the green book like a greedy child on Christmas morning, Roni opened her own book.

Flames belched into the air. The hellspider shrieked as fire engulfed it. Cradling the green book, the hellspider skittered up the wall onto the ceiling, smoke trailing off its burnt limbs.

Roni shut the fire book. If her hands had been burned as before, she did not feel it. While Gram took care of locking down the damage created, Roni kept her focus upon the hellspider.

At first, she thought the creature would open the green book and inhale the smaller hellspiders within as it had done previously — heal before it went on further. But the hellspider had had enough of Gram and Roni. With a slight limp, it gingerly worked its way across the ceiling until it reached the crevice from which it had come. Without hesitation, it crawled in and disappeared deeper into the caverns.

For several minutes, Roni did not move. She stared at the hole in the ceiling, and she breathed. She might have spent hours in that position, but rain fell upon her. The arrival of cold water upon her face snapped her attention away from the ceiling. Gram had opened a book of rainstorms and used it to extinguish the few books that had caught fire after Roni's attack.

Carefully, Roni descended, making sure not to send any more books spinning to the floor, causing more problems. By the time she reached the bottom, however, she had a new focus for her concerns.

Before Gram could say a word, before she could touch her cross or offer a conciliatory smile, before she could raise an eyebrow or cross her arms over her large chest and glare down, Roni lifted an index finger and pointed it at her.

With a sharp scowl, Roni said, "This is all your fault."

# CHAPTER 17

Neither woman spoke a single word as they handled the remaining books. Roni sifted through the piles, separating out the unchained books and stacking them for Gram to deal with. Thankfully, the majority had managed to stay closed — many had retained most of their chains, and many more were difficult to open at best. They resisted. Feeling the covers pull back against her grip, Roni pictured a muscular arm on the inside looped around a ring bolted to the cover.

As she watched Gram working, she wondered if some of those chains could create that resistance. Or perhaps, whoever created the books themselves could imbue them with different properties of strength.

After an hour, Gram chained the last book. Without any acknowledgment or word of any kind, she turned on her heels and walked back through the tunnel toward Sully and Elliot. Part of Roni did not want to follow. She knew what was expected of her, and that alone made her not want to comply. But thinking about the books and their creation only served to increase her frustration over Gram's leadership.

As they trudged through the tunnel, as stone gave way to subway tile, Roni struggled to put her thoughts in order before she spoke. It would have been difficult under any circumstance, facing down Gram had never been easy while growing up, but part of Roni's mind remained back in the courtroom filled with books. They were now chained down. They were secured. But none of those books — at least, none that she was aware of — came from that room. Many of them had been stolen from other parts of the cavern. Didn't they have to be returned?

She supposed not. At least, not by them. Few of those books, if any, had originally been placed by Gram and the Parallel Society. Many would have been secured by other groups from other universes. They had done their part to protect the cavern and those universes held within the books. Perhaps it was somebody else's problem to get the books back where they had originally been stored — if that was what was required.

Perhaps that was simply more evidence of Gram's poor leadership.

By the time they entered the small junction with benches, Roni had worked herself up enough. "You are not facing up to reality," she began.

Elliot and Sully lifted their heads, their expressions revealing joy at seeing their teammates again yet shock at the scowls they witnessed. Sully got to his feet and opened his mouth. A swift gesture from Gram silenced him. She whirled around, taking the center of the room.

"Until just over a year ago," Gram said, "you didn't even know what reality actually was."

"And now I bring fresh eyes to this reality. Or maybe other, more seasoned Society members may have simply grown complacent."

Clearing his throat, Elliot said, "Your hands are injured.

Come. I will heal them. I promise I am not too weak for that small task."

Roni hesitated, but mentioning her burned hands, only ignited their pain once more. Trying to maintain a position of strength on her face, she settled next to Elliot and put out her hands. He lifted his cane to the side of her hands and began motioning a curious circle over her injuries. In seconds, she could feel the pain subsiding.

Though she already felt the fire of their speech dwindling, she knew it was important to continue the argument. Even if in a calmer voice. "I have no doubt you have been a fine leader to this group for a long time. But by your own admission, you brought me into all of this because I am the future of the Society for our world. There's an implication to that — the idea that you've passed your prime in that position."

"Ladies," Sully said, with a grandfatherly smile and a gentle waving of the hands. "The two of you are family. There is no need to fight. We can talk about this and —"

Gram arched an eyebrow toward him. "I need you to do what you're best at. Build us a golem."

"With what?"

"Stones, of course. Lord knows, there are enough around."

Gesturing to the meager pickings on the floor, he said, "I suppose. If I had a pickax, I could make a real golem, but with just the loose rocks, it won't be much."

"Make do."

Roni said, "Unless fire is an option."

"It's not," Gram said, whirling upon her granddaughter. "You would know that if you spent your time focusing on your job and not trying to do mine."

Roni tried to stand, but Elliot tapped her shoulder with his cane to keep her in position. She twisted her head to give Gram a sharp look. "You're not doing your job well. After Elliot's injuries, we should have stopped. It's that simple. When we got to this room you split the group — another bad decision. And when you and I spied the location of the hellspider, we didn't go back to regroup, strengthen up, and come up with a plan. No. We bumbled in there and nearly got killed. Your Ahab-like obsession nearly cost all of us our lives unless Sully could find his way back on his own. And no offense, but I don't think he's up to the task."

Sully chuckled from the floor where he piled stones into the shape of a man lying on the ground. "I think none of us would be up to the task of getting back on our own. Except perhaps Elliot."

Holding her commanding position, Gram glared down at Roni. "By the foolish look on your face, I can see you are still wondering about why Sully can't make a fire golem. Think about it, dear. How is he going to write his spell on a piece of paper and stick it in a golem if that golem is just going to burn it all up? It would kill itself."

Roni slouched back against the wall. As Elliot's hand motions changed direction and pattern, she was reminded yet again that she had no powers. Apparently, she didn't even understand the basics. But that didn't mean she was wrong.

Jutting her chin toward Gram, she said, "Just because I don't know every detail of being in the Society doesn't mean I can't assess your leadership."

"They say everybody's a critic."

"So now I'm a cliché?"

"No, dear." Gram said. "You are just young and inexperienced. Your heart is in the right place. That's worth a hundred people who know all the rules and details. But that does not make you the leader you will need to be. The role of the leader is so much more than simply barking out orders and gaining a benefit here or there." She raised a hand though Roni had not intended to speak. "It is my job to make sure the team is at its most effective level. It is my job to make sure the team is at its best readiness. With the fact that there are sometimes years between events requiring our attention, I have to stay on these boys to make sure they keep practicing their abilities. I have to learn and stay up on the best tactics and military strategies. I'm also responsible for monitoring the entire world, looking for anomalies that might require our attention. That's not all. I also act as a liaison between the Parallel Society and the few religious leaders and government leaders out there who know of our existence. When we have to travel abroad, who do you think is responsible for all the legal hassles involved? It's not like it's an easy matter to take a book containing an entire universe inside it across borders. And that doesn't even touch the surface of what I must do. Because sometimes we end up in a situation like this — out in the field, dealing with an adversary we know nothing about. It is my job to stay a few steps ahead, to improvise, and always, under all circumstances, to make the hard call." Gram's stern look faded, and briefly she warmed into the grandmother Roni had grown up with. "You know I love you. That never changes. And it's with that love that I tell you, you are not ready yet."

Roni did not respond at first — a good leader did not speak rashly. She weighed Gram's words, deciding which ones were worth responding to, and most importantly, what response would sway Sully and Elliot to side with her point of view. With the Old Gang staring at her, waiting, she felt like a defendant on a witness stand. Perhaps even an unfortunate soul forced to sit in that hard, stone chair in the courtroom.

At length, she said, "The Parallel Society is an old institution. It is vital to our survival. All institutions develop traditions, behaviors, cultures of their own. And the longer an institution exists, the more complicated and ingrained those traditions become. They become rules. While they may have begun for a noble or practical purpose, nobody knows why it is still done — other than habit. In other words, just because you've always done something a certain way, doesn't make it right. You taught me that last bit."

Gram's mouth tightened into a small dot. She never liked having her own words thrown back at her.

Roni went on, "I understand and respect that you have a lot to teach me. I know that. But it is clear from the risks you have taken with our lives on this mission that some leadership skills are no longer at your fingertips. Or perhaps it would be better if I said that the leadership skills you utilize have not changed with the times. Decisions you have made on this mission, that you all seem to act as acceptable, should not be."

As Sully wrote Hebrew words on a piece of paper, he said, "You have to pay attention to experience. Experience can be the wisest teacher."

"I agree. But too much experience can lead one into thinking they know all the answers. Which is just as dangerous as not knowing enough."

Sully chuckled. "You got me there. However, I'm still with your grandmother on this one."

"Of course you are." Roni pulled her hands away from Elliot and stood. To Gram, she said, "It's abundantly clear to me now that this is and always will be your team."

Dropping her hands, Gram said, "This team belongs to us all."

"Let's not pretend. This is your team. And that's fine. In fact, it makes everything clear and easier to deal with. This is your team, and one day you want me to take over and be leader of a new team. In order to do that, I need to become a leader, and that won't happen under your tutelage. After seeing the way you've handled our lives in this mission, I'm not sure I can survive long enough to become a leader. I think I'd be better off as a team of one for now, and in the coming years, I'll find others out there, people who can replace you guys when the time is right. I will train them to work under me just like you did with Sully and Elliot."

"Stop it." Gram's stern face had returned. "You're acting like a child, not a leader. How do you expect anybody to follow you if the moment things become difficult, you bail out?"

"You bailed on us. You let us down. I suggest you help the rest of your team to safety, while I figure out how to deal with the hellspider on my own."

Roni didn't wait for a response. She blustered off, fuming more than she felt. In fact, she felt very little anger now. She had let most of it go. It had flooded out in words that she knew she could not take back. She believed most of them — that much was good. But not all. The idea of taking on the hellspider alone did not seem wise. On the other hand, she had no team, and the creature had to be dealt with. And after all, leaders had to make the tough calls. This was her first. She would find a way to take this thing on.

After two minutes of walking she realized she had not gone back down the long tunnel toward the raft. Nor had she gone toward the courtroom filled with books. This was a new path. And as she reached a T-junction, she decided to pause and regroup her thoughts.

Looking the way she had come, the urge to rush back into her grandmother's arms and blubber for her forgiveness had to be beaten back with the hard knowledge that any step in that direction would forever destroy her chances of moving forward toward her leadership position.

"Well, that sucks."

She heard a repetitive thumping coming through the tunnel. Perhaps Gram hurried after her to welcome her back, to suggest that Roni had made an important point, and that she was ready to help her granddaughter learn. Perhaps the Lord would strike down the hellspider and save all of humanity with a magic arrow of love. Roni figured both scenarios held the same likelihood of happening.

The thumping grew louder but did not sound threatening. Moments before it appeared, Roni smiled as she realized what came her way. Sully's golem jogged out of the dark until it reached her. Shaped like a person with two legs, two arms, torso and head, the golem Sully made from nearby stones had only enough material for it to reach Roni's stomach.

Patting its head, she said, "Looks like I've got a team of two."

# CHAPTER 18

Bending down, Roni spotted two divots in the head of the stone golem that reminded her of eyes. She wondered if Sully could give his golems the ability to see through such markings. Possibly.

"You may be a little fella, but you're with me now. I'll do my best to take care of you."

With stone stumps for hands, the golem pounded its chest twice.

"Oh, I guess you like that idea. I do, too. I suppose I should give you a name. How about Rocky? It's a bit on the nose, but I'm in charge here. I might as well go with my gut. Rocky it is."

As before, Rocky pounded its chest twice. Roni chuckled and straightened her back. She gazed up one route and down another. Neither direction called to her as a sensible way to go.

Gazing down at Rocky, she said, "How about you decide which direction?"

Rocky backed up a few steps and considered both paths. The longer it took to make a choice, the more Roni wondered if it could weigh the decision. After all, how much brain function could a stone golem have? It didn't have a brain. Yet Roni had seen Sully's golems in action before. Many of them appeared to exhibit thought and free will.

Punching the air to the left, Rocky jogged off in that direction.

"Wait!" Roni walked in the same direction, pleased to see that Rocky had stopped until she caught up.

They entered a low-ceilinged section of cavern. Stalactites connected with stalagmites giving the sense of pillars sporadically placed in this open hall. Roni traced her fingers along the ceiling as they walked. Chained books fit snug into carved ceiling alcoves. Each one hummed with energy, creating a low frequency of tones that bordered on the musical. It was like standing in a Tibetan monastery while every monk used a different, single tone as his mantra.

At the far side of the hall several tunnels broke off in different directions — some even curved downward. As before, Roni allowed Rocky to pick one. They walked into the new tunnel, and the humming subsided. But it left behind a strange sensation like a residue of sound upon Roni's skin.

She had experienced an overwhelming number of new things on this journey — new creatures, new universes, new concepts of existence. Now humming books. Were they harmless? Or had she just been exposed to something dangerous? Perhaps even a form of radiation. Better leaders would have ensured the upkeep of the Grand Library so that such knowledge was always at members' fingertips. That would be a future project under her leadership. But she couldn't really blame Gram for that problem — it had been one she inherited from previous leaders. Which made Roni wonder what other problems she stood to inherit when the Parallel Society truly came under her control.

Calling Rocky back, Roni settled on a protruding boulder. It had a natural, banana curve that begged for her to rest against. "You know, the real problem isn't the Old Gang or even Gram. I was lashing out at them. I was angry. And, to be honest, I'm more than a little scared." She nodded at Rocky as if the stone golem had spoken. "I know. Hard to believe. But they just won't put themselves in my shoes. If I had learned about all of this, if I learned about things like you, if I had known any of it while growing up so I could be prepared, then perhaps I wouldn't feel so smothered and unqualified. But I received no training, no teaching, nothing to set me up to succeed. I was just thrown into it all."

Rocky walked to the opposite wall and crouched down on its haunches.

"You think I'm going to be rambling on for a while? Maybe you're right."

Rocky put out one arm and made a rolling motion.

"Okay, okay. I'll get on with it. The point is I was unprepared, and yet I was expected to behave like I had been one of the Society for my whole life. Gram wants to be the leader and to set down the rules, and I am to be obedient and blindly follow. But I can't. I have to be responsible for the entire planet, the entire universe — which don't get me started on that. I have so many questions on how we're supposed to handle things beyond our own planet and nobody has given me an answer to that. I've even started looking in the books of the Grand Library and nobody has answers to give me written down or otherwise. That's why I'm so mad. It's not that I want to be off here on my own, but I already am. I already was. They float around me like ghosts — like they're there, visible, but they won't give me anything of substance."

Rocky plunked its head down between its arms.

"Too poetic or am I boring you?" Roni's tone snapped Rocky's head back up. "That's better. What's the point of having a little golem of my own, if you're not going to pay attention? Look, the real problem for me, for all of us, is that the truth is coming after us. I don't mean that like some metaphysical answer, or some spiritual answer, or even the number forty-two. I mean that before I learned about all of this, the truth was a certain reality I understood. And then I discovered the caverns and the Parallel Society and all of it, and now the truth is something different. It's more truth. And seeing the way things have been run here, the way things have been set up to avoid getting too deep into these caverns, the way Gram has dealt with the hellspiders and other relics from other universes — well, I think there's a further level of truth that even the Parallel Society has not witnessed yet. That's what I feel coming our way."

Roni grew quiet, and after a few minutes of silence, Rocky popped to its feet. Nudging her leg, it gestured for her to follow. It then led the way further down the tunnel. Roni did not think her golem friend had a specific destination in mind, though it seemed to move with purpose.

"You smell something?" Of course not. It didn't have a nose. "I mean, do you see something?"

Rocky kept a steady pace ahead.

As Roni followed, her mind wandered back to her earlier words. This was more than some kind of performance anxiety, something an athlete might experience before a big event. It wasn't a simple matter of self-doubt. Of questions like *will she be ready?* Or *will she be capable?* Too much riding on her ability to make the right decisions. And what of the Yal-hara? Wasn't that the ultimate truth? They had a duty to that living relic.

Roni did not truly care if she had to wait to lead the group. She didn't really want it in the first place. Deep down, she felt she was better off alone. But Yal-hara was counting on them.

No. Once again, Roni tried to evade the truth.

The truth — the real truth — was that she did not care who led the group, or what happened to Yal-hara, or if the hellspiders were freed or imprisoned. She had not come down here to impress Gram or convince her grandmother that she was capable of greater things. Perhaps on some level those things existed in her mind, but none of that scratched the real truth.

She stopped walking. Without looking back, Rocky stopped as well.

"I did this," she said, needing to hear her voice, "because I want to get whatever help the kyolo stones will provide for my lost memories. And now that I have the stones, I want to get back to Yal-hara and have her deliver on the promise."

And there it was.

Not only had Roni spoken the truth, but she knew that it rested at the core of all strife between her and Gram. More than any fight over leadership, she suspected Gram would hate the idea of Roni remembering.

Why?

She never had a suspicion of Gram. Her grandmother never once said or did anything to suggest that there were secrets to be hidden. Gram was not a bitter woman, and though tough, she did not seek out confrontation or drama. So why would Roni instinctually feel that Gram did not want her to remember?

If Roni wanted to look at it from the point of view of love, then she considered that Gram worried the discovery might be upsetting — perhaps, devastating — and so she wanted to spare her granddaughter. Yet after discovering her entire reality was false and learning of the incredible, bizarre nature of true reality, there really couldn't be anything in her mundane memories that would shock her. If, on the other hand, Roni took a cynical viewpoint, a darker one, then perhaps Gram knew more about her mother's death than she had let on. Perhaps, Gram had been involved — even if only tangentially.

Roni shook off these thoughts. She had the kyolo stones, and they would hopefully reveal something of her memories. When that time came, Gram's place in all of it would be revealed. No point in working herself up now when she had no knowledge of the actual answer.

"And I better remember that Yal-hara made no promises. She only suggested the kyolo stones might help." Roni knew from a lifetime of disappointment not to grow too excited about the possibility of getting her memories back.

Stretching her arms, she looked back the way she had come. She heard the *thump thump thump* of Rocky running up to her side. Tugging on her arm like a little child, the golem gestured deeper in the tunnel.

"I'm coming. I'm coming."

Rocky's urgency did not cease. Then Roni heard the deep, foghorn moan. Her skin prickled.

# CHAPTER 19

The blood pumping through her system froze in place. She could not move. How had the hellspider found her when she didn't even know where she was? And why? Did this creature seek vengeance? Was that possible?

As her thoughts roiled her stomach, a feather fluttered within her — a glimpse of a memory from her Lost Time. Her father.

They sat in a park. The one that backed up against the Olburg Elementary School. He looked young, fit, ready to be the best version of a dad one could ask for. Several children played on the jungle gym, and though Roni wanted to join them, she could not move.

Her father stroked the back of her head. "Fear is a funny thing. See, in one way it's one of our most important instincts. It is something so basic, so part of us, that without it, we never would've survived long enough to evolve into human beings. But the modern world isn't filled with lions and panthers and things that are hungry to eat you up. So when we're threatened, those two ideas come into conflict — the new world reality versus the old world instincts. And for a lot of us, our body does not know how to react. We shut down. We freeze. Here's the thing — it doesn't matter what you do when you're afraid. It's only important to do something. Don't allow yourself to stand still. Even if the choice you make is the wrong one, it'll be better than standing there waiting to be destroyed."

From what she could remember — and that was, of course, not much — her father often spoke to her like this. He took something as simple as being shy around new kids, and turned it into some big lesson far beyond her capability of understanding at that age. Standing there in the cavern, she got the sense that he might have been trying to prepare her for moments like her current one.

Even as she pushed aside that notion, she realized the memory was right — she had to do something.

With Rocky close behind, Roni hustled along the tunnels until they returned to the low-ceiling cavern. She scanned the area with its numerous paths — which one had they come through?

"Any idea how to get back to Sully and the rest?"

Rocky lifted its head to check all the possibilities. Then it checked them again.

"Guess I shouldn't expect too much from somebody with rubble for a brain." The ceiling hummed with its many books, and when the low moan of the hellspider echoed into the chamber, Roni could feel vibrations in the air rippling off each book.

"We definitely can't stay here. When that hellspider gets closer, I don't want to see what kind of damage those vibrations can do."

Bouncing her finger from one direction to the next, she ran a quick game of eeny–meany in her head. When she finished, she pointed at a tunnel on the left.

"Looks like that's the one."

She wanted to run, but she knew that would be

dangerous in a dark cavern. Too many opportunities to twist an ankle or break a bone. But she couldn't casually stroll, either. Moving as fast as she dared, she headed along the tunnel with Rocky staying near.

The passageway curved sharp in one direction and then the other like a switchback on a mountainside. Though the walls opened and narrowed, and the ceiling raised and lowered, Roni never encountered a junction or even a branching off pathway. With her pulse beating hard and her heavy breaths bouncing off the walls, the steady *thump thump thump* of her golem created a rhythm to their pace. Beneath it all the throaty moan of the hellspider followed by its distinct clicking continued its threat that soon, very soon, it would arrive.

At length, the passage ended in a space no bigger than Roni's apartment bedroom. Shelves had been dug into the stone walls, and chained books filled them with no apparent order.

No doors.

No tunnels, passageways, or alcoves.

No way out.

The hellspider's numerous legs crunching stone as it progressed through the tunnel grew louder. Roni spun back to face the only direction she could go. *Don't stand still. Don't stand still.* If she returned up the passageway, she would smack right into the hellspider. So, that option was out. A quick glance at the walls and the floor convinced her she could not dig a solution.

Books. If she could find another book that opened up into a world of fire or lightning or anything that would inflict harm, then she could fight back. Rifling through the shelves, Roni did not find a cover bearing the symbol that she had seen on her previous fire book. Nor did she find a symbol that indicated lightning.

But she had no way to know if the symbols on these books used the same language as those on the books from her part of the cavern. Considering that the various groups doing the same work as the Parallel Society came from other universes, it would be a lot to expect them to share a common language. Besides, even if she found the book, she soon discovered that these volumes had been chained numerous times. They barely budged when she tried to pull them.

She did not have the time to start cracking them open in an effort to locate a useful one.

Responding to the latest, and loudest, series of noises from the hellspider, Rocky stepped into the entranceway and raised its fists. Like a deer knowing full well that a hunter stalked nearby, Roni gazed up the passageway even as she inched towards the back of the room. Her mind raced through possible ways to escape — their number were few and none seemed good. Worse, the more she strained for an answer, the more her mind conjured images of her horrid demise. She repeatedly pictured the hellspider disemboweling her, decapitating her, or worst of all, it would open its unhinged jaw and inhale her.

Four obsidian legs reached around the edges of the entranceway to grip the wall. More legs followed, and Rocky took several steps backward to put itself between Roni and the hellspider. Accompanied by that incessant clicking, the hellspider entered the room.

The stone golem launched toward the intruder. Yet even as the hellspider got its bearings, it had no trouble swatting Rocky aside. The golem slammed into a wall of books. Turning its red eyes upon Roni, the hellspider approached.

As her gaze lifted to keep focus on the creature's eyes, her heart sank. She had no escape. She had no weapon.

Her palms grew sore, and when she snatched a look, she

saw that her fingers had clenched into fists. As the hellspider gazed down upon her, she mustered all her inner–strength to maintain her composure. Yes, she was scared. But she didn't have to show it.

The hellspider leaned down bringing its face closer and closer. Roni noted an unpleasant, musty odor — like a horse that had rolled around in its own manure.

She could not say whether the next moment came from bravery, inspiration, or stupidity, but before Roni had formed a clear idea of what to do, her body reacted. She punched the hellspider in the jaw.

Its head wracked to the side and the hairs on its face bristled. The rest of it, however, remained still. As it turned back toward Roni, its red eyes narrowed and an angry huffing flared its cheeks.

With so many legs on her opponent, Roni never saw the attack coming. She had fixated on its face, and the two legs that shot forward came low and out of sight. As one struck the air from her lungs, the other shoved her back against the wall. Then the beating really began.

Roni had taken a punch or two in her life, but nothing could have prepared her for the assault she endured. One leg after another pummeled her body. The hellspider struck her in the chest, the arms, the thighs, the pelvis, and of course, the head. It was a jackhammer attempting to break through her bones. The ferocious beating made it difficult to catch her breath, and she worried she would die of suffocation long before any internal injuries took their toll.

Like a boxer, the hellspider exhaled with each jab thrown. Blood dribbled down Roni's face. Her mouth filled with its coppery taste.

She slumped to the ground, and mercifully, the hellspider let her. In moments she found herself lying flat on the stone floor. Everything burned and throbbed and ached, and she had grown numb to the worst pains — at least, she thought so. She cringed at the idea that sometime soon, the full torrential pain would ignite. Unless she died before that unpleasant moment arrived.

Through swollen eyes and a filter of blood, she watched as the hellspider climbed up the wall and onto the ceiling. It positioned above her, making slight adjustments until it centered directly overhead. Roni thought of old wrestling shows that featured costumed stars like Hulk Hogan standing on the ropes of the ring ready to jump through the air and slam onto their opponent for one final big move.

Roni listened to the crowd. The cheers, the boos — sounds that signaled the end.

Obliging her thoughts, the hellspider hissed long and loud before dropping through the air. She saw its multi-limbed body flip over like a cat ready to land on its feet. But it was Roni's head that the hellspider aimed for. The dark figure grew fast in her view, and she had one flashing thought — *I wish I had gotten to find out what I can't remember.*

That was when Rocky saved her.

The stone golem shot out from the side, hurling its body through the air and T–boning the hellspider. The creature flailed out its legs. Knocked off target, it skidded against the floor to the right of Roni.

Too injured to move, Roni simply watched as her stone golem scrabbled atop the hellspider, throwing a flurry of punches. While Rocky did not have the strength to damage the hellspider significantly, the little golem moved fast. Like a dog overrun with fleas, the hellspider twisted and turned and rolled back upon itself in an effort to rid its skin of this irritating bug. But Rocky would not be deterred.

The stone golem ducked, jumped, and maneuvered every way possible to evade the hellspider's lumbering attacks. As the two creatures wrestled on the ground, Roni felt her consciousness fading.

The hellspider thrust back against the wall in an attempt to slam the stone golem, but at the last second, Rocky dismounted and let the hellspider injure itself. Not wasting a second, Rocky lunged back into the fight. Irritated, angered, and possibly hurt a little, the hellspider pivoted toward the entranceway.

Roni saw the creature slinking down the tunnel with Rocky throwing punches on its back. When she could no longer see them, she could hear them — sounds of stone against stone, hissing and moaning, angry cries and multiple grunts, even as the sounds disappeared.

Roni coughed, and blood spurted from her mouth. With each breath, her chest felt as if somebody stood on her sternum. She wondered if she had broken most every bone in her body. She wondered if she would feel Death coming or if she might simply fall asleep and never awaken.

A tear welled in the corner of her left eye and dribbled back the side of her face. She had never given much thought to dying, but she never thought she would die alone.

# CHAPTER 20

The trickling stream made for a peaceful sound, and the warmth covering Roni eased her pains. In fact, she felt little pain. Concentrating on her feet and working her way up her torso all the way to the top of her head, she discovered only the barest throb. Turned out, death wasn't so bad.

She heard the shifting of cloth and smelled the rich aroma of burnt wood. She knew that smell. Only one man she had ever met brought that comforting aroma her way — Elliot.

Opening her eyes, she saw Elliot's gnarled cane above her. His free hand brushed the air back and forth over her head and down to her belly.

"Do not struggle," he said, with a gentle smile. "You sustained quite a large number of injuries. Let my healing do its work."

She tried to speak, but moving her mouth to form words sent crushing pangs through her jaw.

"Close your eyes. Rest. You are safe."

She had questions, but her exhausted body forced her to obey Elliot's commands. Her eyes closed and her mind shut down. Only for a few seconds — at least, that was how it felt. However, when she opened her eyes again, Elliot sat nearby on a large stone eating an apple.

With minimal effort, she managed to sit up. Gently prodding her jaw with two fingers, she discovered no pain. "You're amazing," she said.

Elliot chuckled. "I have had a lot of practice. I must say, though, you were pushing my abilities. I am not a young man anymore. Please, do not get so torn up again."

"It wasn't something I planned."

They sat in a small crater like a fire pit unevenly dug. A pathway passed above them. The stream — not much more than a brook — entered from a hole in the pit wall, meandered along the ground, and disappeared on the opposite side. Leaning back on her elbows, Roni noticed her stone golem standing on the path, keeping guard at the entrance way.

Elliot nodded. "That little fellow saved your life more than I did. It brought you here. Probably dragged you, even carried you, and set you down by the stream. He tucked you in close to the wall so that the hellspider would not easily find you. Then that little golem ran back to us."

"Amazing it found you. We were a bit lost."

"I suspect it hiked every tunnel until it found the right one. By the time it brought me here, you had been gone for six, maybe seven hours."

"Then why are you the only one who came? Something happen to Gram and Sully?"

"They got into an argument. When the golem reported to Sully, we knew that we were partly responsible for your situation. Sully blamed Gram, and she did not take it well."

"I can imagine."

"The two of them can bicker for a long time. I figured it would be better if I came here alone and took care of you right away." Setting the apple core aside, all mirth left

Elliot's face. "That is not accurate. They are not bickering like they often do. They are fighting about you and your welfare. Whether you realize it or not, we all love you very much. I fear the Society is falling apart."

"I'm sorry."

"It is not your fault. The cracks are in our foundation." His throat convulsed as if he fought back the urge to throw up. "The fault is mine."

"I doubt that."

"You are wrong." Resting his cane across his knees, Elliot turned his head away and focused on the stream. "When I first came out to the Book on the Isle, I thought I had made a discovery akin to the Fountain of Youth — something so profound that it would upend all our understanding of the universes. Of course, I could not share this with the world, but for us few in the Parallel Society, I could impart what I learned. Think of the wonder of it all. A world of shimmering beauty. A culture built on love and hope and strength through community. These are things we give lip service to, but the people of that universe truly lived. Arguments are not a bloodsport. Business is not war. If one thing benefits the individual, then it can benefit all. But when I returned with this incredible paradigm shifting news, my words were dismissed."

"Gram can be that way."

"It was more Sully's doing. I think he feared I had succumbed to a Siren call. As it turned out, he was partially correct."

"You went back?"

"First chance I had, I left our world and entered that wondrous place. The people living there welcomed me in without hesitation. They threw a feast in my honor, and the evening stretched on as if it had no end. So much of it blurred together. Songs and dancing and laughter. By far, one of the most joyous nights of my life. And then, right by that fountain, I met Janwan. I fell in love with her immediately. It was not simply an infatuation. It was like meeting part of myself and knowing instantly that we belonged. She was the daughter of one of the town elders — Dorarnosk. I had more than a little fear when I met him. Big man. Full of muscles. But I soon found out that he was a kind and warm-hearted sort. The moment Janwan confirmed that she loved me, I became part of the family. All had fallen into place. All was well."

"Until?"

Squinting upward, Elliot cleared his throat. "A golem appeared."

"From Sully?"

"Who else? It came with a letter — Sully and Gram wanted to remind me that I had a job to do. I wrote back with two sentences: *I can be replaced. Go on without me.* But a few days later, another golem arrived. A few days after that, another. And another. And another."

"Hold on," Roni said as she pictured the scene. "How did they find you in the first place?"

"A map, of course."

"But —"

"I am not some adventurous explorer like Waterfield. I would never have gone walking through the dark caverns nor braved the river currents without knowing where I was going. No, I had a detailed map that he had drawn. But, and please do not be angry with me about this — you see, I destroyed it. I have always had an excellent memory. Still do, even at my age. So, I knew I would remember the route. Sully and Gram, though — I figured they would not be able to find me or send golems after me, if they did not retain the map. I returned for a weekend, gathered the last of my things, destroyed the map, and returned to my wife.

"I thought that would end it all. Gram would find a replacement for me, Sully would get over his disappointment and eventually come to understand, and I would remain in paradise with the woman I loved. Except that woman knew me better than I knew myself. After a year, she convinced me that I needed to return to the bookstore, that I needed to set things right with Gram and Sully, and that only then would I be able to truly live in peace.

"She was right. And if it had gone as she had laid out, I would never have the burden of guilt that weighs on me daily."

Elliot paused, and though he attempted to hide it, Roni spotted him pushing the tears from his eyes. She got to her feet and approached him. The bruises on her body caused the barest of aches. Gesturing to her ease of movement, she said, "You're more than the team's medic. You're a freaking miracle worker."

Shaking his head, Elliot said, "I couldn't save Janwan from cancer."

Roni lowered to Elliot's side and leaned her head on his shoulder. "I loved Aunt Jan so much. I hated seeing her decline. But, if you don't mind me asking, why didn't your skills work? It couldn't have been her age — she was only in her forties or so when she died."

"I tried, but as I have since learned, I need to know the anatomy of a creature in order to heal it."

"Wait — Aunt Jan wasn't human?"

"Patience. We are getting there."

"I'm patient, I'm patient. Get on with it."

"Shortly before we left for Pennsylvania, her father visited with me. Now, Dorarnosk could intimidate a lion, and even though I came to know him as a good man with a gentle soul, I knew he could rip me in two, if he wanted to do so. When dealing with such a powerful man about his daughter, it is always wise to be cautious."

"Is that your way of saying you were crapping your pants?"

Elliot snorted a laugh. "Not literally, but yes. Anyway, Dorarnosk met with me in private and begged me to leave Janwan behind. She would be here, waiting and in love, should I return. Of course, I'll return, I told him, but he insisted that I could make no such promise. In fact, he told me that he knew if I left with her, that she would never come home again. I was confused and a bit worried. How could he know? I had seen and experienced enough strangeness to be open to the possibility that some people might see into the future. But still — I found it difficult to accept.

"I said as much and he laughed at me. No, he could not see what tomorrow would bring, but he did know about the caverns and the great many universes. You see, Dorarnosk and the town elders were that universe's version of the Parallel Society. However, where we have chosen to use our abilities to close the fissures into other universes, capture them in the books, and fight back all the relics that slip into our world, Dorarnosk's group had a different approach."

Roni straightened as she understood. "They built the island."

"They did. They worked the caverns until they built up the land enough for an island. Then they flooded the place, captured their own universe in a book, and stowed it safely alone on the Isle. This would keep them out of contact from the other universes — except for the occasional visit from the likes of me."

Thinking of the hellspiders, Roni said, "Doesn't look like their plan worked."

"Isolation rarely does. Not in the long run. But back

then, Dorarnosk had no reason to believe the end of his
world was only a few decades away. He was simply a father
who did not want to lose his daughter. And he had done his
job to protect their world. I told him that he should
understand then — I had a duty to the Society. I had to
return and make sure that somebody qualified could replace
me. I had to set things right — not only for the sanctity of
my friendship with your grandmother and Sully, but also to
complete my job, to make sure that our world was in good
hands from the encroaching worlds.

"Dorarnosk said he understood that fine, but he also
knew that when Janwan experienced the vastness out there
— all the universes, all the people and creatures — there
would be too much to keep her interest. Why would she
want to return home? I tried to explain to him that his
home was a true paradise, that while Janwan may be
intrigued by our world or some other world, she would
soon find out that her home was the best place to be. Not
so, he told me. People always want to move beyond where
they are. Once they taste the rich possibilities, they forget
about their homes. Maybe not long ago, not when people
were few and the worlds spread far apart, but now — he
knew in his heart that she would not return. So, he asked
me to make a promise. A simple one really — just that I
watch over her, protect her, do all I could to provide her
with a good life. Of course, I made the promise."

Roni wanted to ask a few more questions — namely, she
wondered if Janwan ever learned of the promise or if she
ever regretted leaving — but she could see how difficult
this story was for Elliot to tell. Best to keep as quiet as
possible and let him speak.

"We left shortly after." His voice tightened as he went
on. "I did all I could to fulfill my promise. I tried to give
her a happy, good life. In some way, I believe I succeeded.

But in the end, pancreatic cancer had its way. In another life, I would feel no guilt over that fact. People get cancer. It is the way things are. But not in all worlds. Cancer does not exist in the world she came from. I thought she would be immune to our diseases the way a cat and a human do not share the flu. Different species generally do not get sick from the same things. And while we were both humans, we came from different universes. She should have been fine. And it is not as if cancer were a contagious disease. She should not have become sick. I will never know exactly what happened, but my guess is that her DNA altered after living here for so long. Perhaps if I had stayed in her world, my DNA would have altered. Perhaps I would have been the one to get sick.

"But I learned then that the only way I could heal cancer or any such illness would be to know the person's DNA — the full code."

"And that's kind of impossible."

"It seems unlikely. Certainly impossible for me." He sighed. "Well, it happened the way it happened. She got sick, and she died. I returned to face her father. The moment he saw me, he knew. I dropped to the ground and begged his forgiveness, begged him to give me some way to make up for thinking I knew better. He cried and walked away. And then, before I left, I made the situation worse. I did something which shames me — I stole a hairpin. A piece of Janwan's life from before she met me, before I lured her away and destroyed her. I took this object to our world, creating a relic. Gram was not pleased."

Roni couldn't help but let out a sharp laugh. "I'll bet."

"She made me promise to return it. And so, for the second time, I promised. But time drifted onward, we had missions to accomplish, and Gram had her stash of relic alcohol. I never felt too bad about holding onto a memory for so long. When you brought up the idea of going to the Book on the Isle, I took it as a sign that I should fulfill my word."

"Except you were too late."

"I should have listened to Gram and rid myself of the relic immediately. I should have listened to Dorarnosk and encouraged Janwan to stay in her universe. They knew more than I did, had experienced more, but my youthful arrogance led me astray."

Roni stiffened. "Are you saying I'm arrogant?"

"Nothing wrong with arrogance. At times. We need that kind of surety to be bold. But it can go too far. It can make us believe we know all the answers. But do we?"

"I never said I knew everything."

"Good. Then you will understand that while I agree with you regarding your need to be better educated in the world of the Parallel Society, I do not agree with your running off. Sully, Gram, and I have a lifetime of experiences to offer. We are the greatest textbook you could have to learn your trade. Most of all, you must accept that the tasks we are assigned are far greater than anything we can do alone. The Parallel Society has always operated as a team because a team is the only way to protect our universe. You need to respect that."

"I do. I always have. Heck, my little team with that golem proves it. I would have died without its help. Which, I suppose, means that I need to thank Sully, too. But see, that's the thing. I'm not really a part of your team."

"That is not true. You have made yourself to feel that way."

"A year. A full year and none of you went out of your way to share anything with me. I won't argue this again. Whether you all agree with me or not doesn't change things."

"Then what are we to do? You see now that you need to be with the team — I hope — so, rather than run away again, tell me what we can do to make this work better."

Roni jolted as Elliot's words sunk in hard. On her feet, she spun to face him. Ideas layered atop one another with increasing speed. "You're right. I do need to be with a team." She beamed at him. "But the Old Gang ain't it."

"That is not what I —"

"We can win this. We can defeat the hellspider. Come on. Get up. We've got to go see the others. I know what we need to do." The thoughts racing through her mind threatened to overwhelm her.

"At least tell me what you plan before I go walking all the way back. If we know Gram is going to refuse you, then maybe we can —"

"Stop doubting me. I know what I'm doing, and Gram will agree."

"She will not let you go find a new team."

"That's why we're going to make one."

# CHAPTER 21

Stepping back and forth over the stream, Roni paced the sunken area. She had wanted to rush back to the junction, but Elliot insisted she stay — she still had healing to do.

"Besides," he said, "when the stone golem informed us of your injuries, Gram and Sully headed back for the raft. They went for food and supplies and were to meet me here."

The fact that they had yet to show bothered Roni. But Elliot promised they were fine. He pointed out how long the tunnel to the raft had been, and as extra insurance, he sent the stone golem back to retrieve them. There were a lot of twisting turns in these caverns, and the little guide might be what they needed at the moment.

Twice, Elliot attempted to get Roni talking about her plans. But she dissuaded him — she only wanted to go through the arguments once. She then pointed out that they could take this time to make a more hospitable place for their meeting. Elliot agreed.

Together, they cleared away many of the rocks and stones and found other busywork to kill the time. As they lugged across four of the larger, flat stones to be used as seating positions, Roni prepared for every argument she could think of — every objection, every debatable point. Gram would not like this, yet Roni saw it as their last chance to save whatever relationship they still retained.

With the meeting area set up, Roni and Elliot fell into thoughtful silence. It did not last long. Within minutes, the *thump thump thump* of Rocky announced their guests' arrival.

Ready for the fight to begin immediately, Roni was shocked when Gram entered with tears wetting her face. The old woman scurried down, her arms open and her face betraying grandmotherly love. She wrapped Roni in a strong hug and patted her down at the same time as if to ensure that all the body parts were where they belonged.

"Are you okay?" Gram said holding Roni's head between her hands. "Is anything still broken? Did Elliot do a good job for you?"

Stomping his cane once on a stone, Elliot said, "Of course I did."

Pulling away from Gram's hands, Roni smiled. "I'm fine. Elliot did a wonderful job." Looking over her shoulder, she added, "And thank you, Sully. Your little golem is the real hero."

"Happy to hear it," Sully said, lowering his face to hide a bashful grin.

Before this reunion could derail Roni's plans further, she gestured to the meeting area. "Please, everybody have a seat. We've got some important things to discuss."

She saw the change on her grandmother's face — a hardening, a closing off of the warmth and love to be replaced by her wrinkled stoicism. No matter. That was the face Roni had expected to deal with originally.

As the Old Gang settled on the stones, Roni gathered her final thoughts. Her mouth tasted stale, and she wondered how long it would be before she could once again brush her teeth. Nobody ever mentioned such things about their long exploring journeys. She made a mental note to add such suggestions to her journal.

Looking from Elliot to Sully to Gram, Roni made sure she had their complete attention. "Facing the hellspider on my own, with nothing more than a short stone golem, has made it clear that being part of the team is vital."

Gram snorted. "Any of us could have told you that."

"Please. Let me speak. Because, well, my experience also made it clear that we were never a team."

"Don't be ridiculous. The three of us have been a team for decades and you've been with us for over a year."

"Gram!" Roni's fingers rolled into tight fists. "Not another word."

Her tone sent a shockwave across the room. The boys sat straighter, and Gram's eyes widened as her mouth tightened into a dot.

"This mission started without a team," Roni continued. "I was the one asked to go find the kyolo stones. Not the team. I was the one who did the research, and I pretty much intended to go do the whole thing on my own. Of course, I now know I never would have succeeded, but the point is that I never felt part enough of this team to bring it to you. Elliot joined me, but not the Society, just the two of us. And even we had different missions in mind. I sought the stones, technically for Yal-hara but really I want them because her assistant indicated that I might be able to access my memories with their help. Elliot, on the other hand, cared nothing about that mission. He wanted to return to the Book on the Isle, the world the love of his life came from and where the people he had hurt resided. He sought their forgiveness, and more importantly, he wanted to return the relic he stole."

Roni paused, and she smiled inwardly when Gram did

not take the opportunity to speak up.

"As we tried to leave, the two of you showed up," she said, gesturing toward Gram and Sully. "You bullied your way into our mission, joining without being asked, and Gram took over as if we were all one united group."

"I did not," Gram said, crossing her arms tight. "I am the team leader, and I saw half of my team leaving on a mission that had not been sanctioned. I knew enough about how pigheaded you could be, so I didn't dare try to stop you. But as a responsible leader, I could not let the two of you go off without support. That's why we were there."

"It doesn't matter why you think you came. That's not the point."

Placing his hand on Gram's back, Sully said, "She's right. We were not asked to join, and though I agree that you and I had the best intentions at heart, we have to admit that there really were three teams along on this journey — Roni, Elliot, and the third team, you and I."

Before Gram could get started again, Roni spoke louder. "After we reached the Isle, after we had entered the book and discovered the horrible truth of what the hellspiders had done, our missions were over. I have acquired the kyolo stones I sought, and Elliot found that there was nobody left to apologize to. He buried the relic and bid his farewell. But now we had the hellspider to contend with — a new mission that none of us wanted. And it's in a part of the cavern that probably isn't even our jurisdiction. Yet here we are."

In a strong voice that suggested not only agreement but also encouragement, Elliot said, "You have done an excellent job of detailing out how dysfunctional we have been. And as you point out, the hellspider is out there. Whether or not we have jurisdiction, as you put it, does not matter. We are here, and it is our duty as members of the

Parallel Society to protect the caverns — thus, protecting our world."

"I absolutely agree. That creature is out there and it must be stopped. We all now know that it will take a functioning team to succeed. So, I propose we do just that — form a new team. One that works. The four of us can come together as new. I tried to be part of the Old Gang, but I'm not. I wasn't there for all those decades, going on adventures with you, facing terrible creatures with you, and celebrating victories or mourning our defeats. I can't be part of that. It's too far set in stone. But, if we agree now to form a new team, then the four of us can reorganize and begin our mission against the hellspider as one."

Lowering her hands, Gram said, "How do you propose we do this?"

"We start over as equals. No history, no assumptions based on past missions, we forget what we know of each other, and give each other the benefit of the doubt. Now, I'm not talking about some fairytale amnesia or anything like that. What I am suggesting is that we rely on each other's talents and ignore what we assumed to be true about each other. The three of you think you know me. But you don't. You can't. I barely know myself — how can I, when part of me is missing? You think you know each other, but you don't. You only know each other in terms of the Parallel Society. If we can give each other a clean slate, I think we'll be on our way to forming a strong team together. And our first step towards that must be electing a new leader." She didn't want to, but she couldn't help it — she looked right at Gram. "Not you, not me, not unless the team decides it."

With robotic motion, Gram turned her body to look at each of the men. They shriveled under that stark gaze. Roni did not blame them. Change was always difficult. And in

the case of the Old Gang, the three of them had well–
defined roles to play. Gram had led for so long that the idea
of willfully giving it up was a purple cat riding a dinosaur —
it made no sense.

But Roni believed that certain instincts could override
the comfort of habit. In this case, the instinct of survival.
"We can argue about this all day. You can try to intimidate
the boys, but none of it will change the situation."

"I was not —"

"You might not know you did it, but you did. It doesn't
matter. The fact is that none of us will get out of here alive
without the others helping. We have no choice but to form
a new team. It's up to the three of you. You decide. Either
give up your old way of seeing things, of doing things, of
the way you think, or we die. What's it going to be?"

With her accusations plainly laid out, Sully and Elliot
looked at the ground. Gram stared at them, perhaps
expecting one or both of them to turn to her, to ask for
forgiveness, and to pledge their support towards her. Then
Gram's face changed. It softened. Not as before — not
filling up with grandmotherly warmth — but rather with
understanding. Roni could not believe her words had
changed these three titans of her universe.

She could almost see Gram's thoughts as if they were
written in a bubble over her head — *the Society comes first.*
She saw Gram watch the shame on the boys' faces, and
Gram seemed to recognize her role in the current situation.
Probably didn't want to admit that Roni had been right, but
part of her clearly accepted the truth of Roni's final
statements.

Patting her chest, Gram said, "Okay. I agree. Let us
form this new team."

Sully and Elliot nodded as well. They tried not to exude
relief, but there was no mistaking the change.

Elliot walked over and put his arm around Roni. "You are a smart and brave woman."

Sully clapped his hands. "Here, here."

"Boys," Gram said. "Let's not inflate this girl's ego." Sully and Elliot chuckled, but they also ceased with their praise. Gram continued, "Since we're going to start a new team, then as has been pointed out, we need a new leader. So who's it going to be?"

Not wanting to lose momentum, Roni jumped in. "It seems to me there is only one good choice." She pointed to Sully. "You're the only one who's been impartial in this whole mess. I came for the kyolo stones, Elliot has a whole personal history with the Book on the Isle, and Gram had her own mission in all of this as our previous leader. You, however, have done nothing but support us all. For that matter, I would not be alive at the moment if not for your little golem."

Sully pushed his glasses up his nose. "I don't know about this."

Elliot laughed. "I agree with Roni. You are the best choice. And you would hem and haw for hours if given the opportunity to weigh this decision out. It is a good thing you are not the one who gets to decide who leads."

Gram added, "You have my vote, too."

"Then it's settled," Roni said. "Sully is the leader of this new incarnation of the Parallel Society."

All eyes turned toward Sully. Smacking his palms against his knees, the old man stood with a grunt. "Very well." He walked over to Roni and gestured for her to take his seat. "I will accept."

Gram chuckled. "Oh Lord, I think I feel a little relief. It's kind of nice not being the one in the hot seat anymore."

Sully smirked as he thrust his hands into his pockets. Standing with his slight stoop, he reminded Roni of a politician — not the sleazy kind, but rather somebody like Churchill who could rally the troops and get an entire country behind him. She hoped.

"The first mission of this new group is obvious," Sully said without a hint of shaking in his voice. "We must either imprison or destroy the hellspider. I would like to hear from Gram and from Roni details about the previous two attacks that you were involved with."

As Roni opened her mouth to speak, Gram puffed. "I don't want to tell you how to do your job, dear, but as the only one here with true experience leading, I must point out that going over what we already know is only wasting time. That hellspider is out there, and it doesn't need to go over everything to figure out how to come after us."

Elliot sat up to the edge of his rock. "You are not the leader anymore. Sully is. If he thinks it is worth our time, then we will go over the details of the previous attacks. Besides, you were the one who taught me that it never hurts to take the time to organize thoughts and actions."

Gram stared at Elliot, her eyes wide, her head pulled back, and one hand unconsciously reaching toward her cross. "I was only trying to offer a suggestion from my experience. But if our new leader sees things a different way, then that is the way we will do things."

With as much detail as she could recall, Roni went through the events as she had witnessed them. She told of the way they had first encountered the hellspider in the courtroom. She outlined the way the creature moved, how it disrupted all the books, how it suffered from fire, and how it inhaled the smaller versions of itself. She went on to share her recollection of the second assault. As she detailed the abuse she had endured, she caught Gram cringing. It always felt good to see the grandmother side of her come out — even if only for a moment.

When she finished, she looked toward Gram. "Did I miss anything?"

"Not that I can think of."

Rocking back and forth on his feet, Sully kept his head down and his brow furrowed. His tongue poked out from time to time wetting his lips. He said nothing.

After a few minutes of this, Gram said, "What are we doing? Is he simply going to stand there or do we have a plan?"

"Patience," Elliot said. "You have never really spent enough time watching him create a golem in his workshop. This is how he thinks. Give him a moment."

As proud as Roni felt for both Elliot and Sully, her impatience matched Gram's. Perhaps it was a family trait. Thankfully, she did not have to wait much longer.

"This room you call the courtroom — it has only one exit, yes?"

"Only one we can use," Roni said. "The hellspider came in and left through a hole in the ceiling."

Sully's head snapped up, and he had a spark in his eye. "I know what we'll do. We'll need more stones, and of course, that courtroom. And unfortunately, one of us will have to lure the hellspider out."

Though nobody said a word, Roni knew that task would fall to her. She would be the bait.

# CHAPTER 22

Roni stood in the middle of the humming cave. It's low ceiling and numerous books lodged in stone pressed down harder than before. She envied Atlas who only had to carry one world. The Parallel Society dealt with so many worlds, so many universes.

Maybe this wasn't such a good idea. When Sully had presented his plan, it sounded strong. Perhaps Roni would have supported anything the old man said — after everything she had gone through to reform the team, part of her didn't want to undermine Sully's newfound authority. Yet if they failed, it not only meant the end of her life, but probably the end of numerous other worlds. That seemed a great deal to heap on the four of them.

But if not them, who? They had not seen another person in the caverns. And while the Old Gang had told her that Parallel Societies existed in one form or another throughout the various universes, she had seen little evidence of it. Not that she doubted them, but those groups were not here. They might be doing great work within their own universes, but that did not solve the problem of the hellspider.

That trouble belonged to the New Gang.

For the tenth time, Roni checked that her laces were tied tight. She did not want to trip while running for her life. Although Elliot had given her a clean bill of health, she wondered how quickly her body could jump back into action. The others had gone through Elliot's healing in the past, and they seemed comfortable and secure with his approval. However, they were not the ones standing in the middle of a cave waiting to be attacked by the hellspider.

All four of them had examined the path Roni would have to run. They cleared away anything that might trip her up — every stone, every root, every twig. With a clean route and a solid plan, everything would be fine. Provided she could run fast enough. And if she couldn't — well, she had memories of her previous encounters with the hellspider.

Naturally, because life loves to be cruel, those horrible memories were the ones she could not get rid of. She could feel each strike to her body, and she could bring to mind the way the hellspider threw her. She could feel the heat radiating off its body. And those red eyes — those she would never forget.

Her father had been right. He had warned her — had tried. But it was difficult to believe words coming from a man institutionalized. And that made her wonder why he was there in the first place. A dark thought entered her mind — could Gram have had her father committed as a power-play? No. Roni didn't want to think so poorly of Gram. Besides, Gram had supported this new gang — with a few harsh comments and some grumbling thrown in, but she did come around. She was not a power monger. It must be difficult, having always been the one in charge, having always had the responsibility — letting go could not have been easy. Gram liked to control things, but she wasn't cruel. Certainly not enough to put her son-in-law into an asylum for all these years. Certainly not cruel enough to deny her granddaughter the chance to be raised by her father.

Her thoughts could not change reality, though. Her father was institutionalized. Yet, he had spoken the truth about the hellspiders.

Strange. She had been a child swaddled in a series of ever-thickening blankets — warmed and comforted by the lies that surrounded her. Now that the truth had been revealed — albeit only partially — those blankets had become a tangled mess which she struggled to clear out of. Only it seemed that each time she threw one blanket away, she found another waiting in its place. Unlike a tunnel of thought that shined light at the end to guide one along, Roni had the distinct impression that when she finally pulled away the last blanket, there would only be darkness.

She smacked her leg — these kinds of thoughts would get her nowhere. She needed to either concentrate on the moment at hand or, if that chilled her heart too much, she should dwell on whatever happy memories she could surface. As she pondered which option to take, the decision disappeared.

She heard the moan.

Once again, its deep-throated rumble caused vibrations in the humming air. Stepping out from behind a wall of stalagmites, the hellspider approached with its head brushing the ceiling. It took cautious steps. Its head turned from side to side as its eyes roved around the cavern.

Good. Roni liked that the creature remembered she could be dangerous. At least, she hoped that's what made it so careful.

"That's far enough," Roni said putting out her hand like a police officer stopping traffic.

The hellspider halted and cocked its head.

Roni spotted the way its feet dug into the ground, ready to launch forward. She heard the way it controlled its breath like an athlete preparing for a difficult maneuver. Inhaling through her mouth to avoid the creatures distasteful odor, Roni said, "You are one ugly mother —"

She had only intended the insult to relieve her stress. But the hellspider reacted as if it had understood her. It reared back and bellowed its foghorn tones. The ceiling shook. The humming grew louder, and Roni's head began to ache. She had no idea what the humming books could do, and she did not want to find out.

She didn't want to hang around to be disemboweled, either. Speaking far braver than she felt, she said, "You haven't killed me yet. Want to try? Come on you ugly piece of crap."

The hellspider roared again, and this time Roni did not wait. She whirled around and sprinted away. From behind, she heard another angry bellowing followed by the rapid-fire pounding of the hellspider's legs.

As she raced through the tunnels, adrenaline poured through her veins. She could see the clear path with ease. Each footfall landed exactly where she wanted it. Sweat drained out of her, and she could taste the blood in her system as if it had to go through her mouth first. Though she knew it was all in her head, it seemed real enough. And anything that encouraged her to keep running, she would take.

When she zipped through the junction, she felt the corners of her mouth creep up. *This might work.*

The hellspider grunted behind. With any luck, it would be more exhausted than she was — so Roni kept running.

Bursting into the courtroom, she saw the far wall moving up quickly. As planned, she put out her arms and kept running. Dear Rocky grabbed hold of her right arm and spun her ninety-degrees, lifted her off the ground, and eased her back down, slowing her momentum until she rested against the right side wall. Less than a second later, the hellspider crashed into the room, skidding to a halt in the center. Three legs pressed up against the stone chair on the platform. As it spun its head toward the back, a large golem made of stone stepped into the entranceway and disassembled into a mound of rocks that blocked the hellspider's exit.

From behind a book pile, Gram stepped forward, planting herself between the blocked exit and the hellspider. In her hands, she held a book with the emblem for fire on its cover. "Remember me?"

# CHAPTER 23

As Gram opened her book, Roni saw the new expression on the woman's face — a mama bear protecting her cubs. Fire streamed out of the book as if from a flamethrower. The hellspider vaulted into the air but did not seek purchase on the walls — instead, it shot backwards, towards Elliot. Though several books burned on the floor, Gram had made it clear earlier that nobody should worry about putting them out. The books only held the rifts to the universes, they were not the universes themselves. Losing a book only meant that the fissures leading one universe into another would reopen. Not a good thing, of course. But an acceptable loss under the circumstances.

As the hellspider soared through the air, Elliot fumbled with the book in his hand. Roni wanted to scream that he should drop his book and use his cane — a weapon he felt far more comfortable wielding. But, after the exertions of sprinting through the tunnels, she had yet to catch her breath.

The hellspider body-checked Elliot, sending them both somersaulting across the floor.

Holding the ribs on his left side, Elliot used his cane to

get back to his feet. Roni wished she could dart across the room, punch the hellspider, and assist Elliot in an escape. But that wasn't Sully's plan. Everybody had a job to do, and everybody faced dangers. This was not the time to defy the leadership.

Thankfully, Rocky did not have a specific task. Roni's heart jumped as she watched the little stone golem leap across the room. Launching off a stack of chained books, Rocky twisted in the air and planted its feet hard on the hellspider's back. Roni didn't know if a stone golem could feel cocky, but Rocky sure seemed overconfident. It knew it had gotten the better of the hellspider once and clearly aimed to do it again.

The hellspider, however, had the ability to learn. Rocky scampered along its spine, dodging limbs and throwing punches whenever it could. But Roni could see the difference — the hellspider did not panic. It did not wrench around searching for the source of its discomfort. It knew exactly what it was dealing with.

Though Rocky's tactics were less effective, they did provide a distraction. Elliot swung his cane hard as if trying to knock the hellspider's head across a baseball field for a home run. The loud crack of cane against bone was followed up with a satisfying groan. But Elliot made the mistake of trying to repeat the maneuver.

As the cane cut through the air for a second strike, the hellspider ducked its head while simultaneously punching out with its front limbs. Elliot shucked backwards into a pile of chained books. The hellspider used its momentum to tuck its head down and roll onto its back. It continued until it had returned to its feet — but Rocky had been slammed hard against the floor. Prodding the golem's legs, the hellspider tested to see if it had killed its little enemy.

Having stones for brains, Rocky did not know to play

dead. The little golem bounced up to its feet, grabbed onto the hellspider's leg, and attempted to crawl up the creature's back.

The hellspider did not flinch. Using two of its legs, it grabbed hold of Rocky and swung the golem hard against the wall. Stones and pebbles smashed out in different directions.

Roni gasped — unsure if the rubble came from the wall or Rocky.

With all the confidence of a well-trained soldier, Gram stepped to the corner across from Roni. "Get into position, dear."

Roni moved before her ears had deciphered the words.

With a voice strong enough to carry across the room and back, Gram said, "Hey! Are you so afraid of me you have to go mess around with all my friends? I'm waiting for you." As the hellspider glowered at Gram, she whispered to Sully, "Get moving."

The hellspider stepped towards the chair in the middle of the room. It kept its focus on Gram, moving forward with tentative steps. Sully scooted across until he reached Roni.

"You holding up okay?" he asked.

"I'll be fine."

To Roni's right, a small pile of rocks had been pre-set in place. Sully grabbed these rocks, and surrounded Roni's feet with them. One by one he placed them until they formed a mound up to her ankles. From his pocket, he removed a piece of paper with Hebrew writing. He then closed his eyes and whispered some guttural words into the paper before folding it into a small square.

Handing the paper to Roni, he said, "You won't become a golem. Just put it in your pocket or on your belt, someplace where it won't get lost."

"Doesn't it need to be in the stones?"

"Only if I want it to be alive. But not for such a short and mindless task. Don't worry. You'll be fine."

Roni wasn't worried — not about that. Placing the paper in her back pocket, she felt the rocks on her feet compress as if an invisible hand had tightened her shoelaces beyond what was comfortable. Sully scrunched his brow. "Something wrong?"

"Hurry. Go help Elliot."

Nodding vigorously, Sully hastened along the room, staying close to the wall. Roni had never seen such doubt in Sully's face before — but then, he had never been the leader before. Looking at Gram holding a showdown of will with the hellspider, Roni wondered how long it would take until their new leader had such confidence.

Perhaps she had been wrong to oust Gram. The fearlessness in the cold-blooded strength of Gram could not be mastered in only a year or two. She had spent a lifetime learning how to be the anchor for her team.

No. It was too late for second-guessing. Besides, if they had not put Sully into the leadership position, he would never have come up with this plan.

The hellspider's eyes twitched as it glanced at Sully scooting along. Roni didn't have to say a word. Gram opened her book and the flames singed one of the hellspider's front legs. As the creature sidestepped the flames, favoring its other legs, Sully hustled the rest of the way to Elliot.

Roni bared her teeth. The hellspider had finally noticed its situation. It wanted to turn around and see what Sully and Elliot were up to, but it didn't dare take its eyes off of Gram. Though stuck in the middle of the room, it appeared to have figured out that Gram posed the only immediate threat.

But Roni was no idiot — soon enough, the creature would decide that it could no longer stay still. If it did not act, it would be captured. As Sully piled rocks on Elliot's feet and handed him a piece of paper, Roni picked up the first of the books stacked at her side. This one bore the symbol for a hailstorm.

Sully stepped away from Elliot, turned around, and nodded at Roni. The time had come. With the hellspider's attention on Gram, Roni had plenty of opportunity to lift her book up and aim it at the creature's flank.

She opened the book.

Rocks of ice machine-gunned out of the pages. The hellspider bolted away and Roni tried to follow, strafing the ground with hail. The hellspider scurried up a tall hill of books, out of Roni's range.

Not until she closed the book and glanced over at Gram did she know if their diversion had been successful. To her relief, she saw Sully finishing the stone shoes at her grandmother's feet. Catching Gram's eye, Roni offered a nod and a wink. Then Gram's face fell.

Roni understood immediately. She had taken her eye off the enemy. The hellspider raged down the book hill, stampeding toward Roni. With her stone shoes locking her to the ground, she could not escape.

She opened her book again but the tumultuous storm inside had dissipated. Never can trust the weather. She glanced at Gram, her eyes begging for help. Gram held back. She had no choice. If she opened her book, the flames would have burned Roni as much as the hellspider.

A tear slipped from Roni's eye right before the hellspider bowled her over. It knocked her back with such force that her ankles, lodged in their stone shoes, audibly cracked. She wailed as quakes of pain rippled up her body. A part of her brain heard the scrabbling feet of the hellspider as it climbed the wall behind and dashed toward the blocked entrance. It jumped back to the floor, appearing to understand Gram's hesitation, and turned toward Roni — it knew it was safe from the fire book.

Through blurred eyes and excruciating torment, Roni knew no such security. The hellspider moved in on her.

# CHAPTER 24

When suffering pain — extreme pain — Roni knew the body could numb itself. Whether through shock or adrenaline or some other process she had never heard of, the body could will itself pain free — at least, temporarily. As the hellspider towered over her and pulled back a leg with every intent of mashing her skull, she awaited that relief from her body.

A rock flew in from the side and clunked against the hellspider's head. As it rolled its shoulders to look where the attack came from, another rock flew in smacking directly on its forehead. Several feet away Sully pitched another rock at the creature.

"Varsity pitcher, Hemsdale High, 1964." Like a pro, Sully wound up and pitched another speeding rock.

Gram switched books and opened a new one. As if unlocking a door into outer space, the open book vacuumed in everything it could grab. The hellspider slipped several feet before it could dig its claws into the floor. Books lifted in the air and pulled off the walls but all now had chains locking them to solid stone. They stretched and waved in the winds but none were lost into the vacuum.

Roni's body tried to slide but her stone shoes ended up swinging her like the hand of a clock. She howled in pain. One hand snapped out to grab the nearest part of the stone floor, desperate to stop her body from moving. If only she could be rid of these shoes.

*Idiot!* With her free hand she patted around her pockets until she found the paper that Sully had given her. With her teeth and one hand, she unfolded it twice and then ripped it in two.

The stone shoes crumbled apart. The individual rocks that had formed it rolled off towards Gram's book.

The relief of being freed met with new sensations of electric fire as her broken ankles shifted to new positions. Ignoring her own screams, Roni rolled onto her stomach and used both hands to claw her way toward the wall.

She dared to glance over her shoulder. Rocks and debris flew through the air each one falling into the vortex of Gram's book. The shrieking winds were matched by the clatter of debris. Only inches from her feet, the hellspider clung to the ground, desperate to find its way to safety.

For an instant, the horrifying idea that the creature might leap forward and clasp onto her ankles filled Roni's thoughts. She could see it with disgusting clarity. The large beast had the strength and mass to fly through the air for a moment. Its weight would slam upon her ankles causing high voltage to spike up her legs. The strong vacuum of Gram's book would eventually overtake the creature. But it would not let go, and in the end, it would rip Roni's feet off her legs. Then, if Elliot could not move fast enough, she would bleed to death.

But the hellspider had a different idea in mind.

With the same forceful leap Roni had envisioned, it jumped forward and *over* her — not with the intent of clasping onto her legs, but with the desire to latch onto the wall. It succeeded with two legs.

As it attempted to pull the rest of its body against the wall, the shift in position changed the pull of the book. Roni felt her body lifting off the ground, and she dug her fingers in tighter.

"I can't hold on!"

Gram shut the cover and the winds died immediately. The hellspider scaled up to the ceiling. Rolling on her back, Roni gasped for air. Sweat salted her mouth.

She watched as the creature headed for its old escape — but as it reached the crevice, another stone golem, one as big as the golem blocking the entranceway — crawled out. The hellspider backed up and hissed. The golem did not move. Instead, it disassembled itself, locking its pieces in place to seal the crevice exit.

Propping up against the wall, Roni cringed as she saw her limp feet hanging at wrong angles. As the hellspider crawled across the ceiling toward the center of the room, Roni looked towards Elliot. She wanted to hide her desperation, wanted to exude bravery, but the chemicals in her body that numbed her pain would soon be wearing off. She knew in the long run she should not become reliant on a healer, but she promised herself that she would start her self-reliance on the next mission. Just please save her feet.

Elliot caught her eye. With the motion of his hand and a single, soft nod, he assured her that when the opportunity came, he would do his best to fix her. But there was still the hellspider to deal with. Turning her attention toward Sully, she heard the change in his voice before she witnessed the cold calculations on his face.

"Everyone get ready," Sully said in a near monotone. "This is it."

Gram said, "You sure you want to do this?" Her tone

did not convey doubt in Sully's plans nor did she challenge his role as leader. Instead, Roni heard authentic concern — a sense of foreboding as if Gram knew that making this decision would forever change her good friend.

Sully paused to gaze up at the hellspider. "We tried to capture it, and Roni is hurt. There's no more time. We have a plan for what to do if we couldn't capture it, and that's where we are."

Kissing her cross, Gram said, "Okay." She set down her book and lifted a different one — one bound in red and black leather.

In the far corner, Elliot picked up another book with a similar binding. Sully walked back toward the open corner and picked up a book of his own. He planted his feet hard on the ground, rooting them as if he were made of stone. With each team member stationed in the four corners of the room, all eyes turned up towards the ceiling.

"Roni?" Gram said from across the room. "You sure you're up for this?"

"Don't have a choice. Let's get this over with before I pass out."

Pride flashed across Gram's face before she turned her attention back to the hellspider. She opened her book.

The force with which this book began to pull in the room's air made the previous vacuum nothing more than an afternoon breeze. Taken off guard, the hellspider plummeted to the ground. Before the book could take it away, the hellspider positioned itself behind the chair in the middle. It griped its many legs onto the stone backboard.

The strong winds knocked Roni to the ground. She rolled forward and only stopped when she remembered to slap out one arm to brace herself. She silently vowed that should she survive this, she would invest in some training on fighting, falling, and other important skills.

The book — she had the wrong one. The red and black volume she needed sat atop the small pile only a few feet away. With the wind howling around them and pages fluttering through the air, Roni attempted to inchworm toward her book pile.

The hellspider held onto the chair with amazing strength, but it did not know Sully's plan. Part of Roni actually felt sorry for the creature. She muscled her way further toward the book pile, but she did not know if she would make it before passing out.

Over the roaring winds, Gram yelled, "I can't hold this all day. Sully, get started."

Though Roni could not see Sully from behind the pile of books, she could hear the change in noise and feel the change in air pressure as he opened his book. In an instant, there were two vortexes of energy pulling into two different books. The howling winds shifted to a shriek or perhaps it was the noise of the hellspider. Grasped by these new winds, the hellspider tumbled toward Sully. Panicking, it flailed its legs and managed to scramble back to the chair. Clinging all of its legs around the stone, it lifted its head and cried out.

Roni reached for the book pile and rolled onto her back, panting. She slipped the red and black book off the top and let it rest on her belly. No way could she crawl back to the wall, push herself up, and open the book. She would have to roll onto her stomach and hold the book open from the floor. But without the stone shoes to secure her, she did not think she would last long.

Grunting, she lolled to her side. Elliot raised his book, and as he opened the cover, he met Roni's eyes — he knew the trouble she was in. But the job had to be done. Their duty to the Parallel Society, to the caverns, to the universe, meant more than any individual. That was what the team was all about.

Opening his book, he created a third harsh vacuum. The hellspider's torso lifted free from the chair and fluttered in the air like a flag in a hurricane. Roni thought she heard Gram yelling something but the competing cacophony of storming winds made it impossible to catch individual words.

And then it happened. Roni slid a few inches.

Clutching the book to her chest, she tried to sit up. No good. Even without the pain shooting along her spine into the back of her head, her body was spent — she lacked the strength to raise herself. As she slipped further toward the center of the room, she could see the deep fear on Gram's face, the resigned sadness on Elliot's, and as she cleared the book pile, she also caught Sully's mournful gaze.

With the force of will, she managed to return to her back. Perhaps she could lift the book and open it, even though her aim would not be exact. She could do her part until one of the other books pulled her to her end. But nobody ever mentioned how heavy these particular books were — she would've had an easier time bench pressing Elliot. However, as her heart sank, she heard a sound cutting through the tumultuous noise — one that caused her blood to pump faster, one that filled her with a scrap of hope.

*Thump thump thump.*

Rocky appeared at her side. The little golem only had one arm remaining and lacked several of the stones that made up its head, but it was here. Wrapping its one arm around her chest it yanked her up and then spooned behind her, using its weight to lock her in place.

Cheering for the little guy as much as for her own relief, Roni set the book in her lap and aimed it toward the hellspider. She paused to think of something cool to say.

But the team didn't need a cool quip. It needed her to act.

She opened her book. The front legs of the hellspider stripped free from the back of the chair and stretched toward Roni. The creature spun its limbs like pinwheels, grasping desperately for the chair, but with all four whirlwinds pulling on this creature in four directions, it could not manage to secure itself. It lifted higher in the air, hovering a few feet above the chair.

With a jerk, its legs splayed out. Roni could see the anguish on the creature's face, as well as its realization of what would come. But as Sully had said, they tried to capture it, tried to send it to a different universe, but it had refused. This was the end of the road.

Roni was thankful for all the noise thundering around her. It saved her from ever knowing the horrible sound of the hellspider's limbs tearing from its body. Though she could watch the creature crying, see its terrified face, she never had to hear its torso pull apart. She never had to hear the awful shrieking rising from her own throat. The image of limbs spinning through the air as the four books sucked up different parts of its body would haunt her long enough.

When the last piece of flesh slipped into Gram's book she slammed it shut. Elliot and Sully followed suit, and Rocky helped close Roni's book. The sudden silence rang in her ears. Only three drops of blood dappled the old chair.

# CHAPTER 25

A week later, Roni sat in her car parked in the lot outside of Belmont Behavioral Hospital. She could still see the hellspider's final moments. After it had been killed and the last book closed, Elliot sprang across the room to fix Roni's ankles. He succeeded. Though sharp stings still shot up her legs now and then, it felt wonderful to be able to drive once more. Heck, walking felt like a privilege.

Elliot promised to give her another healing treatment in a few days which, he guaranteed, would clean up the last of the fixable damage. But he also warned — there were limits. Some damage could not be undone. Some would remain always.

Roni agreed with that — the mental damage alone might take forever to be rid of. And not just for her. The whole gang had barely spoken during the trip back.

Using Rocky as a movable walker, Roni had followed the gang back through the long tunnels to their raft. They launched onto the lake and paddled their way to the Isle. Elliot explained that inside the Book on the Isle they had their way home. He led them through the desolate town, towards Dorarnosk's house. They were all on edge, eyes searching for any sign or movement of the smaller hellspiders. But none were found.

Roni limped as well as she could manage. Her newly healed ankles sparked fierce flames if she walked too fast. Plus, they had to leave Rocky back on the Isle. She had already stepped through the book when she realized her golem savior would not be coming. Sully must have pulled the paper from Rocky because, after all, the golem was formed with stones from the cavern. It could not come back with them. It would be a relic. So, Rocky was no more.

"Over here," Elliot said, leading them to the ruins of a large home. Inside what might have been a private office, Elliot found the book he sought. "It will take us to a different part of the cavern. One close to home. And I know the rest of the way from there."

He opened the book and they each stepped through. That was why Waterfield never provided a map with a non-river path leading to the Isle. The way back started in the middle of an empty tunnel. From there they had a long hike, but within a day they were back at the bookstore.

Roni spent the last several days cooped up in her apartment. Resting. Though each member of the gang created excuses to stop by and check on her, she had mostly spent the time alone. Fine by her. She had too many thoughts to deal with — she didn't need more.

That was behind her now. She had finally managed to sleep through the night without seeing the frightening hairy face with those red eyes bearing down on her, ready to devour her. Driving to the mental hospital gave her something different to focus on, and for that, if nothing else, she was grateful.

Waiting outside would not make any of the day easier or better, though. She knew it. Didn't want to admit it, but she knew it.

Making sure not to take her ankles for granted, she eased out of the car and hobbled slowly to the building's lobby. She went through the process of checking in, chatting with the attendants, and eventually ending up in the visitor's room.

Less than five minutes later, a nurse entered with Roni's father on her arm. She walked the man over to Roni, helped him sit in a plastic folding chair, and smiled. Her father gazed off into the distance, his body thinner than before.

"He said he could do without the wheelchair today, but don't hesitate to call if he needs it." The nurse walked away.

For a few minutes, Roni said nothing. At first, she thought she dwelled in the peacefulness and comfort of simply sitting with her father. But her mind could be tricky, and she soon recognized that she had lulled herself into stalling.

"Dad," she said, the unmistakable tremors in her voice echoing in her head. "I faced the hellspider."

His eyes took a sharp turn towards her.

"It's okay. I'm okay. I wasn't alone. Gram and Elliot and Sully all were with me. The Parallel Society — you know it? Of course you do. Well, we had to go into the caverns on a mission, and we came across that creature. But it's gone. You don't have to worry anymore. We killed it."

He dropped his head to the side and his eyes welled. Pulling in his lips, he exhaled a long breath. With a scratchy, distant voice, he said, "You shouldn't have done that."

"I told you. We're fine." The sound of his voice fluttered her heart. She wanted to reach across the table and wrap her arms around his head, but she held off — he was speaking now, and she didn't want to frighten him back into wherever he hid within himself.

"You shed blood. It's the first step."

"Do you know what you're talking about? Do you understand what I'm saying? You don't have to be afraid for me. I'm part of the Society, and we were able to defeat a terrible monster."

"No. You have begun the destruction of the caverns."

"You've got it all backwards. We saved the caverns."

Her father's arm flashed out and gripped Roni's forearm. His eyes opened wide, and in both tone and word, Roni could see that he was momentarily lucid.

"Get me out of here," he said. "It's not too late. I can help you."

Roni twisted as she tried to free her arm. "You're hurting me."

Rising to his feet, her father inhaled sharply and thrust her aside. As loud as a warrior on a noisy battlefield, he said, "You have done a terrible thing. There will be more. There's always more. They will come and they will destroy." He paced around the room, gesticulating toward the other patients, grabbing papers and throwing them in the air. "It's all meaningless. How can we be expected to know the right thing to do? We are lied to, we are manipulated, and in the end, we nearly die trying to do the right thing which is the wrong thing. Unless it isn't which we never really know."

Two burly orderlies rushed in and wrestled her father into submission. He kept yelling about being betrayed, lied to, and yet knowing the truth. They carted him off toward his room.

Roni did not move. Her heart hammered in her chest as she tried to absorb and decipher his meaning. At what point did his words fall away from truth and into his own dementia? The only thing she could be sure of, the first words — *There will be more.* That rang true because she had thought it herself. The hellspiders would not be the last.

# CHAPTER 26

Two hours later, Roni slid into the booth at the Olburg Chestnut. She tried to eavesdrop on conversations going on around her — anything to keep her mind away from the strange words her father had spoken. She checked her watch. A few minutes early. With a wave of her hand, she called over a waitress and ordered a hamburger.

That had yet to get old. After only a short time spent in the caverns, each bite of real food overwhelmed her senses with ecstasy. The simple pleasures. If nothing else, she had gained great appreciation for the nuances of life — like the succulent flavors of an old-fashioned hamburger.

"It is amazing," Kenneth Bay said. He wore another fine suit but had no cane — apparently it was for show. "One always yearns for the basic flavors of their home."

Roni glanced up at the annoying man. "Do I really want to know what Yal-hara eats?"

"Probably not." He settled in opposite her, smoothing his tie with one hand while drumming his fingers on the table with the other. "On behalf of Yal-hara, I thank you for your service. Now, if you would please complete our agreement and hand over the kyolo stones." His drumming fingers stopped as he turned his hand over.

Roni hesitated.

Before she could speak, Kenneth Bay leaned in. "I understand that you went through a difficult time in acquiring the stones. The caverns have never been the most friendly place. But we cannot help you, if you don't help us. Without Yal-hara, those stones are nothing but rocks to you. And if you are thinking about renegotiating our deal, I strongly advise you not to do so. I have been in this game a long time. You have barely begun. You are nothing but a baby, and I can crush a baby."

"Sheesh. No need to get all dark." She set the bag of stones on the table. As he scooped them up and stood, she said, "Hey!"

Running a finger across his mustache, he gazed down at her. "This isn't hardly enough for Yal-hara or you to get what you desire. Traveling to other universes isn't easy — not when you're alone, not part of a group like the Parallel Society. Don't worry, though. Once Yal-hara has all the ingredients she needs, she'll have everything she also needs for you."

Roni clenched her jaw. She felt her emotions competing — on one side, she was like a teenage girl stood up for the prom, but on the other side, she enjoyed the relief of knowing she did not have to show up at the prom at all. "I suppose I already knew you wouldn't deliver."

"Oh, we will. But there are more items in more worlds that we'll need your help acquiring. This is a good start. Soon, we will call upon you again, and when we do, you can be assured that your efforts will be fully rewarded." He turned to leave, stopped, and looked back. He rested his hands on the table, and brought his mouth close to her ear. "No matter what, do not share any of this with anyone. It must remain secret. Especially from your friends in the

Parallel Society. You failed us before in this regard — blabbing to your team about us. But they will destroy us if given a chance. And, to be clear, when I say destroy, I mean kill. If you don't want Yal-hara's blood on your hands — or mine, for that matter — then say nothing."

He left Roni to sit alone.

# CHAPTER 27

The streets of Olburg were congested this particular day, and Roni circled the bookstore block four times before she snagged a parking space. Walking toward *In The Bind*, her jumbled thoughts and conflicted heart duked it out within her. After everything the team had been through, it seemed wrong to hide information from them. But she had already started working on how to free her father — something Gram was against. Plus, she wanted her memories back — another thing Gram resisted. Perhaps, if she kept quiet for now, it would be best.

Turning the corner, she shelved the debate for a later time when she would have privacy. She entered the bookstore and noted the lack of customers. Gram, Elliot, and Sully sat at the big table.

"Don't look so distraught," Gram said. They had a bottle of gin and a bottle of brandy sitting in the center of the table. "This isn't the first time we've had to close up the store for over a week so we could go save the universe. We always reopen and eventually the customers come back."

Sully tilted back a glass of brandy. "Yes, yes. We've been at this for a long time. You can learn a thing or two from your elders about how to run this place."

"I'm sure," Roni said.

With a wave of his hand, Elliot said, "Come. Join us."

Roni shook her head. The way the three of them sat so comfortably at the table reminded her that there newly formed team had only been temporary. "I have a lot of work to do in the Grand Library."

Sully banged his glass on the table. "Says who?"

Gram raised her hands, palms out. "Don't look at me. I'm not leader anymore — and I don't want the job back."

"Then I guess I'm still the leader." Sully pushed back his chair and stood. "This is the New Gang and you, young lady, are part of it. We're a team and it's time that you acted like part of us. Now get over here and drink some alcohol."

Trying to hide her enthusiasm, Roni sauntered over to the table. Sully gently rocked from side to side — a little drunk, apparently. He slid an empty glass toward Roni.

"We have gin, and we have brandy. Or you can make a disgusting mixture of both."

Roni chuckled. "I guess I'll opt for the gin."

Elliot jingled the ice in his glass. "Smart choice. I find it quite delicious."

"I didn't think you drank."

"There are always occasions which permit one to bend rules."

Gram lifted her glass. "I'll drink to that." After tossing it back, she reached for the gin and filled half her glass with it. Then she poured in the brandy to top it off. "Never mind what these boys say. It's delicious."

Before Roni could pick up her glass, Gram sloshed brandy into her gin. The liquids swirled around each other resembling a weak tea. Sully lifted his glass and tapped it with a pencil until everybody raised their glasses as well.

"While we have much to celebrate including the

formation of this latest chapter of the Parallel Society, now that the four of us are assembled together, we should take a moment to recognize those not with us. To Rocky and all of the golems past and future — fallen heroes, each and every one. May they forgive me for the tasks I ask of them and may they always be remembered as partners and teammates of our group."

"Here, here," Elliot said.

"And," Gram said, "let us not forget to toast Sully for taking on the thankless and difficult job of herding us cats."

"Here, here," Sully said.

"Also," Roni said, surprising herself as much as the New Gang, "let's toast to a new level of honesty between us. Secrets kept from me throughout my life led to unfortunate outcomes. And to me being a bit stubborn."

"A bit?" Gram said, and the boys laughed.

"Perhaps more than a bit. But we can't be a solid team unless we build trust. That comes from sharing information, not hiding it."

"To honesty," Sully said, lifting his glass higher and dribbling a little gin onto his hand in the process.

"To honesty." Elliot knocked back his drink, as did Gram.

Roni took a short swig from her glass. She thought of her father and Yal-hara. And secrets.

The drink burned down her throat.

# ACKNOWLEDGEMENTS

There are always people to mention. Some know exactly how they contributed to a book. Some have no idea they were involved at all. But regardless, these are a few of the many people deserving a mention: the wonderful people at Deranged Doctor Design for the new covers; Lisa Gall, Randy Miller, and the entire Launch Team; the folks who created Dragon Naturally Speaking; and of course, my wife and son.

Last, but most importantly, a big thanks to you, my readers. If you're enjoying this series, please spread the word. I would love to keep writing about Roni and the New Gang.

## RONI AND THE GANG RETURN IN
## RIFT ANGEL

When Roni and Gram head to Ireland to inspect an open rift beneath an Abbey church, they are faced with a strange and dangerous relic. Something alive inside the rift that wants to get out. The Abbey nuns are convinced it is an angel. But Gram harbors a secret about the so-called rift angel, one that haunts her. And soon Roni will learn that the nuns have secrets of their own.

The lies and secrets would be plenty enough to deal with. But when the rift is breached and an angel set loose, Roni will wish she could be back in the underground library!

**Once you've caught up on The Parallel Society, try Stuart Jaffe's bestselling series The Max Porter Paranormal Mysteries!**

From ancient curses to witch covens, World War II secrets to local lore, underground boxing to underground chambers, Max Porter and his team investigate it all.

Don't miss a single story in the bestselling series, the Max Porter Paranormal Mysteries.

**And don't miss this unforgettable stand alone, time travel fantasy**

REAL MAGIC

Duncan Rose, magician and card cheat, accidently slips back in time to 1934. Swindling his way through this new world, he searches for a doorway home, until a ruthless mobster takes notice - a man who wants to use time travel for his own purposes.

REAL MAGIC is an exciting time travel fantasy packed with real card tricks designed specifically for this story by renowned card magician, Cameron Francis.

# ABOUT THE AUTHOR

Stuart Jaffe is the madman behind the *Nathan K* thrillers, *The Max Porter Paranormal Mysteries,* the *Parallel Society* novels, *The Malja Chronicles, The Bluesman, Founders, Real Magic,* and much more. He trained in martial arts for over a decade until a knee injury ended that practice. Now, he plays lead guitar in a local blues band, *The Bootleggers,* and enjoys life on a small farm in rural North Carolina. For those who continue to keep count, the animal list is as follows: one dog, two cats, three aquatic turtles, nine chickens, and a horse. As best as he's been able to manage, Stuart has made sure that the chickens and the horse do not live in the house.

Made in the USA
Las Vegas, NV
31 July 2021